LOVE IN A MIST

When Alice's grandfather is taken into hospital, she moves into his cottage in Lyme. Joining forces with her friend Megan, the two go into business together. But sculptor Tom Carey is furious that they are renting the premises of which he was promised the tenancy. Though Alice dislikes Tom, she finds herself falling in love with him — much to her dismay. Could she possibly have been wrong about him after all?

Books by Sheila Spencer-Smith
in the Linford Romance Library:

THE PEBBLE BANK
A LOVE SO TRUE
THE BREAKING WAVE

SHEILA SPENCER-SMITH

◆

LOVE IN A MIST

Complete and Unabridged

LINFORD
Leicester

First published in Great Britain in 2013

First Linford Edition
published 2016

A catalogue record for this book is available
from the British Library.

ISBN 978–1–4448–2804–7

Published by
F. A. Thorpe (Publishing)
Anstey, Leicestershire

Set by Words & Graphics Ltd.
Anstey, Leicestershire
Printed and bound in Great Britain by
T. J. International Ltd., Padstow, Cornwall

This book is printed on acid-free paper

1

'*What exactly is going on here?*'

Startled, Alice Milner whirled round so quickly that the man standing in front of her appeared through shafts of dizzying light. He was taller than she was, and broader, but she wouldn't be intimidated.

'I beg your pardon?' she said, trying to control the trembling in her voice.

'I want to know what's going on.'

She clutched the cat basket she was holding closer to her. 'I could ask you the same question.'

'But I have more right.'

'I doubt that. This shop is mine since I signed the contract yesterday to rent it for the next six months,' she said. 'So how is it your right to come charging in here, scaring me out of my wits?'

'That's not possible.'

'Oh, it is. You're truly scary.'

His spark of amusement was instantly suppressed. 'So where are the previous tenants?' he demanded.

'Why do you need to know that?'

'I left some work with them before I went away. I can't afford to lose it. Tom Carey, sculptor,' he said, by way of a belated introduction.

'I'm sorry. I can't tell you where they are.'

'Can't, or won't?'

'Do you doubt my honesty?'

His blue eyes glinted at her. 'Since I don't know you, I'm in no position to judge,' he said, in a deep voice that would have sent shivers through her if she hadn't been so utterly irritated at his audacity. 'I have a verbal agreement that I am to rent this place when the previous lease expires. It's my right to be here, not yours.'

'Then how come you weren't aware that it was vacated two months ago?'

'I was out of the country.'

'Enjoying yourself when unfortunate events were unfolding here?'

'Hardly, if it's any of your business.'

Alice felt her flush deepen. She had allowed herself to be provoked instead of keeping calm, but she wasn't going to apologise. 'So you're unaware that the previous tenants were made bankrupt?' she said.

'Bankrupt?' His voice was deep with suspicion.

'There was some sort of trouble. The owner had to re-let or he would have been in financial difficulties. He waited two months.'

'And so you were quick to step in. Illegally. My solicitor will hear of this.'

Suddenly Alice felt too exhausted to argue. 'You must take that up with the owner, but I doubt it'll do you much good.'

'You think not?'

'And now if you'll excuse me . . . '

He hesitated for one brooding moment and then left. 'You haven't heard the last of this,' he called back over his shoulder.

The door crashed shut behind him

and she shuddered as the sound died away in the empty room. Then she pulled the bolt across on the outside door, wishing she had done so when she arrived. But Megan would be here soon — and how was she to have known she would be accosted on their own premises, by someone casually dressed in chinos and T-shirt, looking as if he had come straight from some hot Mediterranean beach?

Her eyes flickered towards Pickles, her grandfather's pride and joy, purring on the windowsill, his black fur glossy in the brightness. He stretched and then leapt off, winding himself round Alice's ankles. She had never known Pickles to be so affectionate and his action now was a surprise. For a moment tears of exhaustion filled her eyes. She dropped his basket, picked him up instead and buried her face in his warm, purring body, taking a deep, calming breath. They had been working so hard since they took over the lease, she and Megan. With her friend's help she was determined the business would be a success, but they couldn't let up for a minute.

'You'll protect me from fierce intruders, won't you?' she murmured as she stroked his thick fur with a hand that trembled. 'Grandad must be so proud of his gorgeous cat.'

She would take good care not to mention the worrying intrusion when she visited this evening. Since his beloved wife died, her grandfather had become shaken and easily upset, and she had tried to keep even the smallest of problems from him. And this sounded as if it could be a big one, for all her act of bravado. Tom Carey, sculptor, looked as if he meant business; and she and Megan Ross, her best friend and new business partner, could have a problem on their hands.

Alice glanced at her watch. So where was Megan? She should have been here by now, staggering in with some of her belongings. When she left their home this morning, Megan and Harry had been loading Megan's car with all the things Alice couldn't cram into hers; it shouldn't have taken her long.

She put Pickles down now on the bare floor and picked up his bed, pleased that he followed her upstairs as if he knew this was to be his new home for the foreseeable future. And her own too now, of course. Already her bed was in position and made up in the back room with the view of the harbour and the sea, and if she stretched her head round a bit to the right, she could just glimpse the high harbour wall known as the Cobb.

There was a small sitting-room, a bathroom and a kitchen that served as a dining-room as well. Here she placed Pickles' basket in the corner out of the way, straightened the cushion and patted it invitingly.

'There,' she said.

Pickles, ignoring her, sprang onto the windowsill, sat with his back to the room and stared out at the view almost identical to that she had from her bedroom.

She smiled. 'Megan will be here soon with the rest of my things, and that includes tins of cat food and your feeding dish. You'll show more interest then.'

The cat's ears twitched and she smiled to see it, filled briefly with the same optimism as she had felt yesterday on signing the lease. But it didn't last. She could dwell only on Tom Carey's air of absolute confidence and control as he'd stood in the empty room downstairs, looking as if he knew he was in the right and was going to prove it with the sheer force of his will.

* * *

Alice and Megan had become friends when they were both fourteen and in Year Nine at Comprehensive. They'd found themselves in the same group for Maths, a subject they both hated. How ironic that, many years later, Megan

7

had married a man who thought that numbers made the world go round, came top of his year in his accountancy exams and now worked in the prestigious firm of Olton and Readey here in town. But definitely useful too. Harry was going to be indispensable in their new project because he would be making sure they were financially viable at all times.

'No fiddling the books,' he warned, looking at them sternly.

'As if we would!' Megan exclaimed indignantly.

He winked at Alice. 'You won't get a chance with me on your case, believe me.'

Megan picked up the nearest cushion and threw it at him. He fielded it expertly and made as if to throw it back.

'Now, now, children,' Alice had said, laughing. 'Behave yourselves.'

It had been good staying with them when she had got back from Crete because there wasn't room for her in her grandfather's one-bedroomed cottage down near the harbour. Megan and Harry were such excellent company and had been good to her these last few difficult weeks, especially when Grandad had been taken into hospital with an old problem that had begun to trouble him again. She and Megan had done everything together as they were growing up. Megan's uncle had a boat he used for fishing trips and he'd often taken the pair of them out when conditions were right. They collected fossils, too, after winter gales had battered the cliffs and caused minor landslides that exposed new areas to search. Alice still had her collection she'd stored in the roof space of her grandparents' home even when they moved to Lyme, just before she took up her job in the tourist office in Crete.

The fossils would look good here in her new place, she thought. Maybe they could put them to good use when decorating the rooms downstairs in preparation for the big plans she and

Megan had been making, and could now put into place. A surge of excitement made her smile now as she thought of it.

Working and living in Elounda on the beautiful island of Crete now seemed like a distant dream from a lifetime ago. She tried to remember how she had felt, waking each morning in summer, knowing that outside her shutters a beautiful day dawned and soon the place would ring with cheerful shouts and the sound of boat engines.

She had loved working there — until the news came that Gran had collapsed down by the harbour, back home in Dorset, and never recovered consciousness. As soon as she heard, Alice packed her most important belongings and got on the first flight possible. She had known immediately that she must stay because her grandfather was no longer in a fit state to look after himself. He needed her now, just as she had needed her grandparents when her widowed mother had been involved in a fatal car crash, leaving her orphaned. She could never pass the site of the accident now without thinking of her young, vibrant mother singing nursery rhymes to her when she was a young child.

★   ★   ★

There was a hammering on the street door and Alice ran down to open it.

'You look relieved to see me,' Megan cried, bursting in with two bulging bags she dropped on the floor.

Alice rushed to hug her. 'And how! I thought you were the bailiffs come to evict me.'

'What for? Trespassing on your own property?'

'If it *is* that.'

'What do you mean?'

Megan looked incredulous when Alice filled her in on what had happened. Her eyes flashed and there was a twist to her mouth that Alice only saw when her friend was livid about something she felt was important.

'You didn't believe him?' Megan demanded.

'Well, no, not really. But he seemed so sure of his rights.'

'And we're sure of ours. Harry will soon sort him out.'

'Harry's an accountant, not a solicitor,' Alice pointed out.

'And the one who encouraged us in this, remember. He heard that the place was empty, and for what reason. He'd have been quite sure of the legality of it, Alice, believe me.'

Alice smiled, reassured.

Megan looked at the bags she had brought with her. 'How about getting the rest of your stuff in? I'm parked on double yellow lines.'

'You'll get caught out one day,' Alice warned.

'But not today,' Megan said confidently.

They unloaded the car between them, and while Megan drove off to find somewhere to park, Alice carried it all inside. Most of her belongings were here now, and later she could get started on the unpacking while awaiting the delivery of a chest of drawers, a table and some chairs. Luckily, there were already carpets upstairs, and the ground floor had only recently been re-floored.

'We'll have to make sure we don't get paint all over it,' Megan said doubtfully when she returned.

'That's my problem,' Alice said. 'You'll be in the kitchen making sure your students aren't throwing food about.'

Megan laughed and visibly relaxed. 'Last-minute nerves,' she confessed. 'I can't quite believe this is happening, can you? I'm feeling a bit crazy thinking we can make a go of something so different.'

'A gap in the market,' said Alice. 'Some financial outlay to start with kitting out the place, and then we'll be on our way. We're OK with that, aren't we?'

'According to Harry.'

They had discussed this long and hard, with Harry on hand to throw in words of advice when needed.

'You get off home for a bit,' Alice said now. 'The stuff shouldn't be long arriving and I'll see it in. Come back this afternoon so I can get to the hospital to visit Grandad. I'll be fine.'

Megan looked doubtful. 'What will you do while you're waiting?'

'First I'll get some food down for that starving cat. Then I'll get things unpacked and sorted.'

'If you're sure?'

'Absolutely sure,' said Alice. 'And sure that our new business will be a huge success. We'll have art groups queuing up to get booked in with us, and for your cookery classes too. Lyme won't have seen anything like it before.'

Megan laughed. 'If you say so!'

★ ★ ★

The place seemed extra-quiet when she had gone, and Alice suffered a moment's doubt about the wisdom of what they were doing. But the rent was paid a month in advance and there was money in her bank account to cover the next few months. It was natural, wasn't it, to have a few qualms at the start of a new venture, human nature being what it was?

The idea had first come to her when looking for a suitable oil painting class to keep her occupied before she found gainful employment, now that she was home. She loved painting the sea in all its moods, and wanted somewhere she could do it in complete freedom with others who felt the same way, whatever their choice of medium.

Megan had gone with her to Dorchester one afternoon to do some shopping while Alice was at the hospital. On the way home, they stopped the car at a lay-by near the highest point on the A35 to gaze over the valley and hills to the distant sea. Along the coast in the distance was the distinctive shape of Golden Cap, slightly hazy in the late afternoon sunshine.

'I want to paint it one day as the sun's setting over the sea,' Alice murmured.

'So do it.'

'I need space for that, lots of it, that's suitable for all my oils and everything. I'll have to wait until I can get my own place.'

'Harry said there's an empty shop with a flat above it to let in Love Street, half way up the hill. It used to be a health food shop, remember?'

Alice was thoughtful. 'Yes, I do.'

'You could work there, couldn't you, and then sell your paintings? I'll come and cook meals for you if you like. It would save my catering qualifications going to waste.'

Alice turned to her, smiling. 'They're surely not wasted on Harry?'

For a moment Megan looked sad and Alice knew why. They had hoped to have started a family by now but it didn't seem to be working out.

Alice turned back to the view she never tired of. 'Imagine that on canvas,' she murmured. 'With a brilliant sunset sky. I'll paint it for you, Megan, as soon as we get ourselves organised.'

'Organised?'

'I've had the most brilliant idea.' She swung round, feeling enthusiasm rise in her like a wave from the sea. 'That place would be the perfect venue for organising art groups. There must be others like me, interested in splashing oil on canvas with no space to do it at home. Oh — and I've got the perfect name! Since it's in Love Lane, we could call it *Love-in-a-Mist*. It was my grandmother's favourite flower. Grandad would be so pleased. What d'you say?'

Megan looked bemused. 'I don't know one end of a paintbrush from the other, and I'm not sure I want to.'

Alice laughed. 'But you're brilliant at baking and things like that. 'Why don't we have cookery classes too?'

'You wouldn't actually be running an art *class* though, would you?'

'Not a class as such. I'm visualising workshops, one or two days a week, for people to come in and do their own thing in complete freedom. And maybe we could get a tutor in once a month.'

'But would that be costly.'

But Alice wouldn't be put off.

'I think it could work,' she said. 'We'd charge a certain amount for, say, a ten-week period; extra for the tutored class, of course, to cover our costs.'

'And show a profit?'

'Of course, if we can get enough people interested. We'll advertise.'

'Harry's always talking about business plans.'

'We'll make one. Now.'

Megan looked round in mock dismay. 'At this very minute?'

'As soon as we get back to your place.'

* * *

That had been the start of it, and Alice was glad to see — for the moment

— her friend's sad look vanish. To her delight, Harry had been interested too and it was he who arranged for them to view the property. He had dealt with the owner, who was desperate to re-let. By this time they had discovered the lawn at the back with the splendid view over the bay and were eager to make a start on their new project.

'We could do cream teas in the garden in the summer months,' Megan had said at once. Now Alice stood gazing out of the back window at the patch of grass that Megan thought had potential. Pickles licked his clean bowl and then wound himself round her ankles, purring.

2

So how was it possible that that a metal sculptor could leave his work in a health food shop, presumably for sale, for months on end? There was something odd going on here because it simply didn't make sense. The strangeness of it had occurred to her as she was packing some of her canvasses to take to the framers later, in Oakley Mill. That sounded odd too, she mused, if you didn't know that Martin of Martin's Framing rented an outlet in the grounds of what used to be a thriving flour mill a few miles inland.

But metal sculptures for sale in a health food shop?

When her grandparents had moved into their terraced cottage near the harbour, just before she'd left for Crete, she had come to Lyme Regis to stay with them for a few days, and had visited the shop for a bottle of the ginger wine her grandmother liked. Alice wrinkled her nose now in an effort to remember, but was sure she hadn't seen any metal objects lurking among the packets of organic flour and vitamins.

'Unless they were too small to be noticed by someone looking for one particular item, of course,' she told the purring Pickles, still entwined round her legs. 'But wouldn't you think they'd have been put in a prominent position to tempt customers to consider buying them? It would have been good business practice.'

So what would the antagonistic Tom Carey have chosen as his subject? Alice smiled as she envisaged metal objects in the shape of exotic fruit looming above the shelves. Or maybe he favoured sculpting back-from-the-brink wild flowers to make a point about harmful insecticides? That would appeal to the owners of a health food shop. But she wouldn't have described

21

him as a sensitive person who cared about wayside flowers being lost to new generations.

Endangered species then, large animals that might in future years have the same fate as those who once ruled the earth . . . mastodons, dinosaurs . . . But wait a minute! It was easy to get carried away here. You wouldn't get a full-size mastodon through the doorway, however hard you tried — even though Tom Carey didn't look the kind of man to give up easily.

Alice had almost forgotten that she was awaiting the delivery of some furniture, and when it came she was still at the window, trying to imagine things made of metal among the products being sold in a health food shop.

'Anyone at home?'

'Coming!'

Alice rushed downstairs as a chest of drawers was being unloaded from the van.

'Where d'you want it then?'

'Upstairs, if that's OK?'

'Right you are.'

They looked too young to be working for a delivery firm, mere schoolboys in their cut-offs and spotless white T-shirts. They were taking the greatest care not to knock into the paintwork and seemed to know exactly where to place the furniture in the room she indicated. Next, the table and chairs that had to be taken upstairs too, and after that six long folding tables for the space downstairs, with twelve folding chairs to be stacked against the wall.

Now things felt as if they were beginning to happen!

When they had gone she finished packing up her paintings, scenes of Lyme she had done on that visit to her grandparents and never had framed, and then went out for a quick lunch. She bought coffee and a salad roll at a kiosk along the seafront, and sat on the low wall that edged the beach of soft sand, to eat and drink in the sunshine. She looked across to the harbour and to the Cobb beyond, wishing she had time to walk out to the end of it. But Megan would be back soon so it must wait until another day.

*   *   *

Oakley Mill lay in a valley, surrounded by green, rounded hills, where sheep nibbled the soft turf and larks trilled overhead. Alice turned right off the lane and bumped slowly along the track beneath trees that soon would be heavy in leaf. Late bluebells brightened the banks, and ahead she caught sight of the old mill buildings, with the waterwheel hanging still and silent above the pool of water.

She lifted out her paintings and sniffed the slightly muddy air. It was so peaceful here, it made her think of a more leisurely time; and yet the years when the mill had been in action would have had their own problems, just as people had today.

People lived, and died, and strove for a living, then and now.

Startled, she nearly dropped her paintings as a gaggle of geese appeared from the corner of the building. Their cackling drowned out the soft murmur of the insects in the grass. Hardly a peaceful scene now, she thought. Smiling, she ignored them and looked towards the low wooden building she had come to visit.

Good, the picture framers was open for business. Martin, the owner, was as helpful as when she had first visited to make enquiries about prices and the sort of frames he could make for her. She couldn't linger today, but she knew what she wanted and her order was soon placed.

Her mobile rang as she was getting into her car.

'Alice?' said Megan's voice. 'What do you think? Our advert is in this week's paper after all, and someone's rung up to enquire about it already. Can you believe it?'

Alice heard the excitement in her friend's voice and responded with enthusiasm. 'That's great news, Megan. You'll stay there till I get back just in case we get more?'

'Harry's coming along later. With luck we'll get all those lovely tables up and into position.'

'Don't work too hard.'

'You know me, as lazy as they come.'

Alice giggled. 'I'm on my way to Dorchester now. See you!'

This was a good start, Alice thought, and something to tell her grandfather that would be sure to please him. He was so anxious for her to make a success of her new life, and weak as he was, he liked to hear every detail about the plans she and Megan were making. It had been good to reassure him that Harry Ross was overlooking their finances so that any worries he might have on that score were put to rest.

★ ★ ★

Alice, about to push a leaflet through a letter box near the Town Mill, heard a sound behind her and turned round in annoyance. 'You're stalking me!'

Tom Carey stood looking at her, his head a little to one side. There was nothing threatening about him now but she was wary.

'No way,' he said pleasantly.

'Then what are you doing here?'

He smiled. 'It's hardly my fault you choose to deliver your post in the same places I happen to be.'

'I'm following a sensible route around town to deliver these.'

'Me too.'

He was impossible. This was the third time she had caught sight of him since she had set out on her self-imposed task after tea. At first she had thought she was imagining his tall figure, in jeans and white shirt like so many others still thronging the streets, but no-one else had that mop of dark curly hair. Tom Carey was definitely keeping an eye on what she was doing,

27

and she didn't like it.

'But you're not delivering anything,' she said.

He glanced down at his empty hands in mock dismay. 'I have to say that you've got me there. But I can offer my help with that lot if you like.'

She frowned. His sudden friendliness was unnerving after their bitter encounter this morning. 'I don't think so.'

'As a peace offering?

Alice looked at him suspiciously. Her contact information was printed on all the advertising they had arranged, and with the answerphone on at the flat and her mobile in her pocket, she wouldn't be missing any calls. But still, she didn't want to be too long at this task. Her unpacking wasn't finished yet and tomorrow they had plans to get the downstairs area up and running ready for the open morning event they had arranged for Saturday. Surely this change of heart on his part was too sudden to be believable, though? Tempting as it was to get the job done more quickly, it was likely that the nearest bin would benefit from an extra load as soon as she was out of sight.

'No, thank you,' she said sharply.

Relieved that he took the hint and left her alone, she delivered her leaflets to the rest of the cottages in the row and the detached ones round the corner, where the road narrowed alongside the River Lyme as it burbled between grassy banks. Instead of following it further she took the steep road up the hill towards the top of the town, delivering her leaflets as she went, until she had posted them all.

And that was enough for this evening, she thought. She and Megan would get the rest done in the morning.

Worn out, she sank into bed later, but sleep wouldn't come for a long time. Round and round in her head was the worry about Tom Carey's earlier threats to prove that the lease of *Love-in-a-Mist* should rightfully be his. He had promised that he would be back, and she had mentally geared herself up for a fight. So was this approach a deeply-laid plan on his part to undermine them?

* * *

Alice and Megan both worked hard for the next few days and by Friday morning the main room downstairs was transformed. The tables and chairs looked good the way Megan and Harry had arranged them, leaving space for the art tutors' demonstrations once a month. Alice had placed her easel there for the moment and on it was a colourful programme of art events and workshops planned for the future as well as Megan's list of classes.

Megan had found a bolt of pretty blue-and-white material and spent a useful few hours at home making cloths, to cover the card tables — surplus to requirements at the church hall — that they had been able to purchase at a good price.

'Just right for our back lawn,' she had said.

So they had placed them there now, just to see what they looked like. Through the large back window they seemed charming.

It had been Alice's job to do the flower arrangements for the window sills inside, to make the place look attractive from the road. Now that most of the preparation had been done, she and Megan stood in the middle of the room and looked round, feeling proud of themselves.

Megan moved one of the tables an inch or two. 'I think we should have more room to display those paintings of yours,' she said.

'I'm not too sure that's a good idea at this stage,' said Alice.

'Come on, Alice. They're brilliant.' Megan looked round as if she expected them to appear at the click of her fingers.

'They're at Oakley Mill, being framed.'

Megan reached for the phone. 'Check if they're ready for collection, then.'

Alice hesitated, but she knew when she was beaten. She took the receiver. Minutes later she put it down again, pleased in spite of her sudden fears. Seeing her work framed was always a pleasant experience, because her paintings always looked so professional, almost as if someone else had painted them. Maybe it was because they had been away from her for a few days, but she didn't think it was only that.

Megan looked at her expectantly. 'Well?'

'They're ready to be collected now.'

'There you are, then.' Megan sounded triumphant. 'Great. Shall I come with you to get them?'

'We need someone here, don't you think?'

'To fight off the hordes of enquirers? You may well be right. Wait till they see your work in the window, Alice, my talented friend. There'll be no stopping them then.'

Alice smiled as she picked up her car keys. 'I won't be long.'

Now, moving purposefully to the door, she told herself not to be so silly about showing her own work. No-one would ever do anything creative if they were afraid of what people would say about it, and that wouldn't be a good thing.

*　*　*

To meet Tom Carey — deep in conversation with the picture framer, Martin, in his workshop at Oakley Mill — took Alice so much by surprise that she just gaped at them both as she went in. It was like a bad dream, she thought, as she replied to Martin's greeting with one of her own in a voice she tried hard to keep steady. The two men seemed at ease with one another, as if they were old friends.

Martin smiled at him, rubbing one

hand down the sleeve of his old grey jersey. 'You've come for those paintings?'

'I'm interrupting,' she said. 'It's OK. I can wait.'

'Not at all,' said Tom, moving back a pace or two.

She glanced at him as he stood leaning on the bookcase, seeming perfectly at home. Did the man get everywhere? This time she couldn't accuse him of following her, but it was odd that he was here.

Martin moved across to the pile of wrapped paintings stacked nearby. 'I have your work here.'

'Thanks for doing them so quickly,' Alice said.

He was a big man, dark-haired, and with long fingers she could imagine working deftly among the wood he kept stored at the rear of the room. Now he searched among the work waiting for collection.

'Business is obviously booming,' Tom said.

Alice ignored him.

'They're here somewhere,' said Martin. 'Ah yes, I thought so.'

He lifted them out all at once and placed them on the counter. He then peeled enough of the wrapping back on each of them in turn for Alice to inspect his work.

'They look great,' she said.

'Not so fast,' said Tom, behind her.

He was harder to ignore this time because she could almost feel his breath on the back of her neck.

'Excuse me?'

He moved to stand beside her and looked down, frowning, at the last painting exposed.

Martin looked at him as if Tom's judgement was intensely important to him.

'What's wrong?' said Alice.

'Whose idea was this?'

'Mine, if it's any business of yours.'

'You asked Martin to frame it like that?'

Martin cleared his throat. 'The

customer's always right, Tom.'

'Not this time.'

'I chose it because I like it,' said Alice.

'A seascape like this deserves better . . . something light to complement the storm clouds, not this dark frame that does nothing for the work at all.'

'You seem very sure.'

'I *am* sure. And so Martin would have been, if you'd given him half a chance to give his opinion. That's so, isn't it, Martin?'

'Enough,' said Alice, incensed, before Martin could answer. 'This is what I chose and I'm pleased with it. And now I'd like to settle up and take them home.'

She was aware of Martin's embarrassment as she paid the bill, and her cheeks felt hot in sympathy. The sooner she got out of here, the better.

Before she could stop him, Tom stepped forward and picked up her paintings. 'Here, let me. They're too heavy for you to manage. Where's your car?'

There was nothing for it but to follow him outside and indicate the only car in the patch of ground set aside for parking. 'Over there.'

Where were the geese when they were needed? A few of them cackling round his legs tripping him up would have been more than welcome, she thought — as long as her paintings stayed safe. But the amount of bubble wrap Martin had used would have made sure of that.

3

Alice pressed her key fob and the click of the unlocking doors was loud in the silence. 'Inside the car itself, I think,' he murmured.

She opened the door, and he took infinite care in placing four in the back and two in the intervening space between front and back seats.

He straightened and looked at her. For a second his smile seemed uncertain.

'And now, if you could move to one side, I'd like to get in,' she said.

'It's not too late, you know. Martin would reframe it for you.'

Did he never give up?

'Are you going to move?' she demanded.

For a moment it seemed as if he wouldn't, but then he leapt to one side.

'Think about it . . . ' he called out, as

she turned the key in the ignition, but the rest of his words were lost as the engine sprang to life.

The lush banks of cow parsley and red campion had no power to enchant her now as she drove along the bumpy track to the lane. Her hands trembled and her cheeks glowed. With a huge effort she had managed to suppress her true feelings back there talking to Martin, but now she knew she would be a danger to other road users — if there were any along this quiet lane. Just in case, she pulled into a field gateway until she felt calm enough to proceed with safety.

The arrogance of the man!

She thought of the painting in its dark frame, knowing it was one of her best: she had caught the sunset glow on the wave tops with a finesse that pleased her. She felt deeply hurt by Tom Carey's criticism of her choice of frame. Fair enough for him to dislike her because he thought the empty shop should have been his. She could understand that. But criticising her choice of frame seemed more personal.

She had set out from Lyme to pick up her work, feeling relaxed and happy that the preparations were in place for their open day tomorrow. But her enthusiasm for that was slipping away fast because of Tom Carey's strange attitude. He had made his intention to fight them clear from the beginning. When it came down to it, he needed their space. She couldn't deny that their failure would suit his purposes only too well. So maybe he was trying another approach now — trying to undermine her confidence in the hope of getting his own way?

A blackbird clacked in agitation and flew low across the lane in front of the car. A moment later it was back again. Alice watched it fly over the hedge and then perch on the branch of the hawthorn near the gate.

She had promised not to be too long because Megan needed to get home. Her friend and partner would be sure to laugh at her for taking such notice of a man who had made it clear he was their enemy.

Alice took a deep breath and let it out slowly in an effort to calm herself. She was wasting her time and energy being unduly sensitive. She set off again, resolved to put Tom Carey out of her mind.

* * *

Megan's outfit next day was eye-catching, to say the least. Alice was in the garden at the back when she arrived, making sure that Pickles knew this was his home now and would come back inside in due course.

The back door flew open. 'Hi there, Alice, all set for today?'

Alice looked at Megan in surprise as she came tripping out to join her in a skirt so short there seemed to be nothing of it.

'Like it?' said Megan, twirling round in heels six inches high.

'It's . . . colourful.'

It was certainly that. Bright red and purple flowers on a background of yellow could hardly be called dull.

Megan laughed as she came to a standstill. 'I thought I should make an impression,' she said.

'Has Harry seen it?'

'What does Harry know?'

'A lot more than you give him credit for.'

Megan grinned. 'All right. You win. I thought I'd try it out on you, my love, that's all. Lighten the atmosphere a bit.'

'It worked,' said Alice, smiling.

'Just my bit of fun. I knew you'd have been up for hours working yourself up into a frenzy.'

'I'm OK now you're here, Megan.' And so she was, Alice thought with relief. She had tried hard not to worry about the success of the day they had planned for so carefully. After yesterday, it had occurred to her that today would provide the perfect opportunity for Tom Carey to show up and make difficulties, but she wouldn't think about that any more.

'Harry's inside with my bag of suitables, and while I'm changing into them he'll get the tables up out here,' said Megan cheerfully. 'And I'll look so boring I'll fade into the background.'

'Not you,' said Alice, smiling.

Megan shivered and rubbed her bare arms. 'It's going to be a lovely day, but it's early yet.'

'I'll get the coffee going. I need it after a shock like that.'

Megan giggled as she tottered beside her in her high heels, across grass still damp with dew. 'It was worth it to see the expression on your face.'

'I was worried that Harry would think he'd married a crazy woman.'

'He does, all the time,' said Megan. 'It keeps him on his toes.'

* * *

The sun was well up by the time the tables were in place, and the water in

43

the bay was sparkling with golden light. In the far distance to the east, Portland Bill was slightly hazy, which was a good sign. The air was warmer, too.

By the time Alice carried out her tray of coffee pot, milk and mugs, Harry had placed all the chairs in position. Pickles was curled up asleep near the back door, his black coat shimmering in the sunshine.

'I'll get the cloths on later,' said Megan, sitting down at the nearest table. 'I don't want you spilling coffee all over them, Alice, and messing everything up.'

Alice laughed and sat down too, the sun warm on her face. She closed her eyes for a moment, wishing her grandfather could see them now, with everything looking so good. He wanted her success so much; with luck, she would have a lot to tell him this evening.

'Shall I pour?' said Megan.

'Feel free.' Alice opened her eyes. It was good to have this time together, she thought, smiling at Harry, who sat there looking cheerful in his maroon sweatshirt and jeans that looked lived-in and comfortable. She was lucky in her friends: Harry, so supportive and reliable; and Megan, such a talented cook, with a lively personality sure to inspire anyone who came today to sign up for one of their proposed classes.

'So,' Megan said, leaning so far back in her chair that it creaked. She raised her mug. 'Here's to the resounding success of *Love-in-a-Mist*.'

'I have every confidence in the pair of you,' Harry said. 'When I come back at four o'clock I expect to see you both ecstatic with the number of people who've signed up for your workshops.'

'And paid their deposits,' said Megan.

'You're not staying, Harry?' said Alice, disappointed.

'This is your show, girls. I'm to help bring in the tins of fabulous cakes Megan's been up all night baking,' he said. 'Then I'm off.'

'Not quite all night,' said Megan, her

voice complacent.

'Where do you want them, Meggie, in the kitchen? Right, then, I'll see to that and then leave you to it.' He bent to give her a brief kiss, smiled at Alice and went striding away across the grass.

Megan watched him go, a smile curving her lips.

Alice sat up straight and drained her coffee, anxious now to have a final check on everything.

'Relax,' said Megan. 'It's all there, ready. What can go wrong?'

'Apart from no-one turning up?'

'More likely, we'll run out of china. Or seats. Or forms for the workshops. Or that greedy cat of yours will drink all the cream, or a tornado will hit the middle of the lawn, or a fire will start in the kitchen, or . . . '

'Stop!' cried Alice, laughing. 'You've made your point.'

'There's one thing, though, isn't there?' said Megan, suddenly serious.

'There is?'

'Your phantom man might turn up

and create a scene.'

Alice leaned forward, frowning. 'He's real enough, Megan, and he might just do that.'

'Harry's only at the end of a phone,' Megan pointed out. 'The man won't know what's hit him if Harry lays into him. What's he like, anyway?'

'Arrogant. Bossy. Interfering. Determined to get us out of here by whatever means.'

'Any bad points?'

Alice gave a hollow laugh. 'Be serious, Megan.'

'What's he like to look at?'

'Tallish; thick, dark, curly hair; athletic-looking and tanned. He said he'd been abroad for six months.'

'Rich, then, or a layabout.'

'He makes sculptures out of metal.'

'Garden gnomes?'

Alice giggled. 'He's not the type for that, believe me.'

'I can't wait to meet him.'

'I can,' Alice said with feeling. 'He'll show up for sure, and create some bad publicity to stop our plans going ahead.

'Then we'll be ready for him.' Megan struggled to her feet and picked up the tray. 'I'll get those tablecloths on now and the coffee ready to go on. Find something to do, Alice, for goodness' sake. And stop worrying.'

Alice stood up too. Megan was right. Worrying herself silly about Tom Carey at this stage wasn't going to make any difference. They'd have to deal with him when . . . if . . . he came.

She had already picked some early roses from the climber on the fence by the back door, and with some of the leaves from the columbines arranged in small glasses, they made pretty little tables decorations that looked well on Megan's blue-and-white tablecloths.

Pickles got up and stretched, and then set off for the far end of the lawn to find a cooler spot to doze. The jugs of cream wouldn't be left uncovered, of course, but it was as well not to leave temptation in his way. Smiling, Alice went to join Megan in the kitchen, just in case there was something that needed doing there.

* ★ ★

By ten o'clock three people had arrived: two young girls in shorts and brief T-shirts, and a boy with a mop of curly hair.

'We came to see what you're doing here,' he said in a lofty tone.

'You're welcome,' said Alice, hiding a smile. He looked so confident standing there, feet apart, that she suspected he was putting on a show for those giggling companions of his, who were unashamedly staring at the tray of cakes Megan had placed on the table near the kitchen.

'On holiday, are you?' asked Alice.

He nodded, eyeing the cakes too. 'Sort of. We're at a good place up the road in a chalet. I'm looking for work.'

'Permanently?' said Megan, her eyes twinkling.

He hesitated.

'We're just starting up, you see, said Alice. 'We haven't an opening at the moment.'

'Go on out to the garden and I'll bring you some lemonade,' said Megan as more people arrived.

'We'll have coffee, please,' he said loftily.

Megan grinned. 'Certainly, sir. I'll be with you in one moment.'

The room was filling up nicely now, with people asking questions and picking up some of the leaflets and application forms. Then the door was held open for a wheelchair and an elderly woman in a bright pink top propelled herself in. Alice rushed forward to help her get settled near the window. She found she enjoyed explaining about the art sessions: two days a week over ten weeks, with a professional artist giving demonstrations once a month — a different person each time. But she couldn't help glancing at the door every time someone else came in.

'Which days?' the occupant of the wheelchair asked, her face alive with interest. 'My son might like to come, but he's at work during the week.'

'It says on here, Suzie,' the man with her pointed out as he picked up a leaflet and handed it to her. 'Wednesdays and Saturdays. That's convenient. I might come along too. Will the numbers be restricted?'

Alice smiled. 'Of course. A maximum of twelve people at a time. You can choose which of the days you want to come. A subscription for the ten weeks is payable on the first day. A ten percent deposit now secures you a place.'

'Fair enough.'

'Twenty pounds a session?' said Suzie, frowning. 'That's a lot, isn't it, Brian?'

'To include teas and coffees and a light lunch,' Alice pointed out.

'A bargain,' Brian said.

Someone else was joining in now, and others were listening too. 'I don't paint at home. We haven't got a lot of space

51

and my husband objects to the smell. I need somewhere I can spread out and experiment a bit.'

'We'll have that here,' said Alice.'

'I've never done oils before. Do you take beginners?'

'I wouldn't know how to start,' someone else chipped in.

'The sessions will include students of all standards,' Alice told them. 'Beginners will find plenty of help because I'll be on hand to make sure they know what's what. In fact, the first session for each group will be a free workshop — just for the morning — to start things off, and for everyone to see how it works. I'm starting a list for those now.'

'Who's to be the first professional demonstrator?'

'Someone good,' Alice said. 'To be announced later.' At this rate she might have to book one very soon, while there was someone still available.

'The same artist who did those paintings over there?'

'They're my own work,' said Alice.

'I'm impressed,' said Brian, Suzie's friend. 'I see they're for sale.' He moved towards them to take a closer look.

'You've got a fan there,' said Suzie, smiling.

Alice glanced across at Megan who was looking a little flustered as she was hurrying in and out with trays of coffee pots. Nearly all the tables out on the lawn were occupied now. Alice took a deep breath as she considered where she was needed most.

Brian came towards her looking purposeful as he pulled his wallet out from an inside pocket.

'I think you've got a sale,' someone said.

'Two,' said Brian above the noise of chattering. 'Those two at the end. Wonderful sunset views of Lyme Bay. I couldn't choose between them.'

'Thank you,' said Alice. 'I'll get some wrapping paper.'

'No need. I'll take them as they are. The car's very close.'

'I'd like to buy one, too,' said a young man in leathers carrying a helmet beneath one arm. 'Let me just get rid of this.'

This was more than Alice could have hoped for so early in the proceedings, and she felt a frisson of excitement as she dealt with money and wrote receipts. There was a lull after this, as some of the people left while others made their way into the garden, where Megan was talking about the baking and cookery classes planned for the Thursday of each week.

Alice went to join her after a quick glance to check that Tom Carey hadn't slipped in unnoticed. Outside, she found the young boy collecting empty cups and piling them on a tray to carry indoors. His forehead looked warm and there was a line of moisture dampening the edges of his curly hair.

'That's good of you,' said Alice.

'She said I could help.'

'We certainly need it today.'

'And on other days?' he persisted.

'How old are you?'

'Seventeen?'

'Twelve, more like,' said Megan.

'Sixteen?'

'We're not stupid.'

'All right then, fifteen. Honest truth.'

Megan nodded. 'What's your name?'

'Danny.'

'We can't afford to pay you, Danny. But if you're that determined to help, feel free — as long as you provide written permission from whoever's responsible for you in case you think of suing us.'

He grinned. 'Chocolate cake?'

'Maybe.'

'You're on.'

'Wednesday then,' said Megan. 'Eleven o'clock.'

★　★　★

'That was good of you,' said Alice when at last they were alone and sitting outside with a coffee pot on the table in front of them and two slices of the chocolate cake Megan had kept back. 'A nice kid. He reminds me of someone.' She wrinkled her nose in an attempt to work out who.

'Good-looking too, with that mop of curly hair,' Megan said, leaning back in her seat and yawning. 'He'll have the girls buzzing round him in a year or two. He won't be so determined to help us out then.'

'But why?' said Alice. 'Didn't it strike you as strange?'

'I was too busy to be struck by *anything*, and now I'm exhausted. What a crowd! A successful morning, wouldn't you say?'

Alice looked at the list she had brought out with her of the people booked in for the free workshop on Wednesday. 'Eleven,' she said. 'That's brilliant. And we've several firm bookings for the Saturday sessions as well.'

'And all your paintings sold?'

'Except one.' Alice's face clouded. The one that had been criticized by Tom Carey for its dark framing when she collected it. She pictured him standing there in Martin's workshop, feet apart, so sure he knew best.

She stared at Megan, aghast. 'You don't think . . . ?'

'What's up?'

'The boy, Danny. We didn't ask his surname. Suppose it's Carey? Oh, *Megan*! When I met that man at Oakley Mill he was too friendly, too quick with seemingly good advice about my painting. I suspected then that he was trying a different tactic to wear us down. There must be some connection between the two of them, and he's sent this boy to see how we're coping.'

All traces of tiredness gone now, Megan sat up too. 'You're over-reacting.'

'I feel I've been duped.'

'Relax, Alice. What can he do, anyway? Our lease on this place is legal, all fair and square.'

Alice knew that, of course, but something wasn't quite right. She was sure of it.

4

The first thing Alice did on Monday morning was to remove the offending painting from the easel in the downstairs window and take it to place against the wall of her kitchen upstairs. Then she went down again with a purring Pickles at her heels and let him out into the garden. She stood, shivering a little in her pink dressing-gown, watching him stalk across the grass towards his favourite place near the escallonia bush in the corner.

Clouds covered the sky and the rising breeze ruffled her hair. In the distance a lone gull's cry broke the silence. Out at sea the horizon was misty and she felt a soft hint of drizzle in the air. Not a morning to linger out here, she thought. But what did the weather matter? Saturday's warmth and sunshine had been important for the Open

Day so that those who chose could wander about outside to admire the view while they drank their coffee. This morning, with Megan's help, she would be inside: deciding exactly how the tables would be arranged, ready for the free workshop morning on Wednesday. In the meantime, the fitters would be getting the new kitchen appliances into position and connecting them in the right places. By tomorrow, all that would be finished and they could get this room ready. With luck it wouldn't be too much of a squeeze. Two people would be able to sit at each long table, with enough space in between for individual easels.

Alice had fed Pickles and was washing up the breakfast things when the phone rang. At the same moment she heard Megan's key in the front door downstairs.

Alice picked up the phone. '*Love-in-a-Mist.*'

'We can't do the kitchen, I'm afraid; not today,' a husky voice informed her.

'What's wrong?' Megan mouthed as she came into the room and discarded her jacket on one of the chairs.

Alice held her hand over the mouthpiece. 'One of the fitters is in hospital. Appendicitis.'

'Tell them to send someone else, then.'

Alice frowned at her and replied to the man on the other end. 'That is bad,' she said with sympathy. 'I'm really sorry for him. And for us, too, of course. We've got a business to run here, you see. We need the work done as soon as possible.'

'We're getting a replacement as quickly as we can, but it'll have to be Wednesday now. It's the best we can do.'

'But I'm holding a workshop here on Wednesday.'

'Sorry love, we're really booked up. It's either this Wednesday, or a week Thursday.'

'Wednesday it is, then,' said Alice, resigned, as she replaced the receiver.

'Wednesday!' Megan cried. 'What are you thinking of, Alice? It's your trial workshop morning.'

'And it's your first cookery class a week on Thursday!'

'But . . . '

'It's OK, Megan. We'll just have to manage.'

Megan snatched up her jacket. 'It's disappointing, that's all.'

'But not the end of the world.'

Megan let out a long sigh and then smiled. 'Come back home with me now, Alice, there's nothing we can do here at the moment. We'll have the morning off. They do a good lunch at The Horse and Hounds. On me, of course. Then you can go straight from there to the hospital to visit your grandfather.'

The offer was too tempting to refuse.

★　★　★

On Wednesday morning Alice was up early to let Pickles out for his morning ramble in the wet and dripping garden. The sky was a uniform grey and everything looked dismal.

Indoors, everything was ready for the workshop — with enough space left between door and kitchen, she hoped, for the men to get the kitchen goods through. There was plenty of time for that before the first people turned up at ten o'clock. Megan would be here soon with tins of her homemade biscuits for the planned tea- and coffee-break at eleven. With Danny to lay out the cups in the upstairs kitchen and carry the laden tray down for her, there would be no problem there.

Alice took a last look round downstairs, then went up for a leisurely shower and to dress in clean jeans and a T-shirt that had seen better days. She hated working in a painting smock or apron, but had made sure in the wording on the application form that the artists — beginners especially — knew it would be a good idea to wear some sort of protective clothing.

After she had fed the hungry Pickles and eaten her own breakfast, she shooed him out into the garden again.

'Amuse yourself today, my lad, and earn yourself a good report for me to carry to the hospital this evening,' she said.

He gave her a baleful glare and marched off.

Smiling, she went indoors just as a vehicle drew up outside, blocking off the light in the main room.

Two men got out, one with a clipboard in his hand.

She flew to open the door.

'Your electrical appliances,' one of them said, consulting his list. 'A cooker to be built-in; with a double oven, hob, extra-wide and . . . '

Already his mate had the back of the van open and was climbing inside. Between them they got the first huge cardboard box out and onto a trolley.

She saw at once that she hadn't allowed enough room for them to get it through to the big downstairs kitchen. Some of the tables needed to be moved further out of the way to clear more space. As the first box was manoeuvred through the door, Alice dragged the nearest table and then grabbed the others to move them too.

'We'll be off, then,' said one of the men when the last box had been brought in.

Alice stared at him blankly. 'Off?'

'The fitters are coming later. We don't do that job.'

'They're definitely coming?'

'If they're booked to come, love.'

'They'd better be.'

When the van had gone, allowing what light there was on this gloomy day to flood back through the windows, Alice sank down at one of the tables and gazed at the wet, muddy floor. The tables would have to be left where they were, crammed far too closely together. The items in their bulky wrappings took up most of the space in the kitchen area. She had her kitchen upstairs to use later for the tea- and coffee-making, but even so, it wasn't how she'd imagined the room down here would be.

The phone rang and Alice leapt up to answer it.

'Have they come?' said Megan.

'The stuff has. It fills the kitchen. It's not unpacked and the fitters aren't here yet.'

'They will be soon, if I have anything to do with it. I'll get onto them when I get there. Leave it with me.'

'Thanks, Megan. You're great.'

'I do my best,' said Megan modestly. 'They won't know what's hit them. Getting nervous?'

'Mmn. A bit.'

'I'll come at once.'

Alice replaced the receiver and took a deep breath. They had been planning for this day for so long, and now it was here. Make or break, she thought. This was it.

★ ★ ★

The fitters arrived at the same time as young Danny. He stood behind them, wide-eyed with surprise, clutching a large hard-backed notebook to his wet jacket.

'You're late!' said Megan, accosting them in the doorway.

'You're lucky to have got this slot, Madam.'

'Lucky!' Megan indicated the tables behind her, where the first arrivals for the art workshop were looking round expectantly for somewhere to hang their wet outer garments. 'It doesn't feel lucky. You can see we're busy here.'

'We won't disturb you,' said the younger man, smiling at her in what he obviously thought was a winning way.

But this didn't work on Megan. She glared back at him. 'How can it do anything but disturb us, you lot crashing about in the kitchen while we're trying to concentrate in here?'

'We'll shut the door.'

'What good will that do?'

66

'It'll help.'

Alice stepped forward. It wasn't an ideal situation, but they had no choice other than to let the men go ahead. Megan needed the facilities in the kitchen before the first of her bakery classes the following week, and this was the only time the fitters could do. 'Will you be long?' she asked.

'That remains to be seen,' said the younger man, who had obviously taken offence at their reception.

'Then we shall have to hope for the best.'

The men nodded and went into the kitchen, banging the door shut behind them. Megan shrugged, and then beckoned to Danny; laden with wet garments, they climbed upstairs to Alice's kitchen to drape them on the chairs and tables up there. Not ideal, Alice thought, but the best they could do.

The atmosphere already felt disturbed as Alice went to the front of the room to welcome everyone and to apologise for the conditions they found themselves in.

'Not what I expected,' someone called out.

Ignoring him, Alice went on to explain how the proposed workshop days would be organised. She had already booked a local artist to come the following week, and for that there would be a special fee. His demonstration would be in pastels, to give them the chance to use other mediums.

Several people wanted to know if they had to pay for the session of ten workshop days in advance. As Alice repeated the information that was clearly set out in the brochure, she was aware of ripping cardboard and loud banter from the room next door, and then the sounds of heavy appliances being dragged across the floor.

A middle-aged man in a red shirt shuddered, and the woman beside him held her hands over her ears.

'Monica's migraine isn't going to stand up to this,' the man said.

Alice was alarmed. 'She has a migraine?'

'Not yet,' he said ominously.

There were some more murmurs from behind him.

Alice raised her voice, explaining that she had flowers and fruit on hand that could be set up as still-life arrangements, and a selection of photos for inspiration.

'I'll be on hand to discuss anything, and to help generally,' she said. 'And I've a selection of oil paints anyone can use, and some spare brushes over there on that table.'

A loud crash almost drowned her words.

*   *   *

Upstairs, the kitchen smelt of wet clothing, and already the windows were so steamed up they could hardly see the rain slanting down from the leaden sky.

'Not a good start,' Megan muttered. 'We'd better get the kettle on and some

69

hot coffee down them before they all decide to pack up and go home.'

'I'll open the window, shall I?' said Danny, springing into action.

'Enjoying this, are you?' said Megan.

'I like a challenge, me.'

So did she, usually, Megan reflected, but they could have done without one today.

'Thanks for coming early,' she said, a little grudgingly.

He grinned and picked up the hand towel to rub his mop of curly hair.

'What's that huge notebook you brought with you?' she asked.

'That? My record book. Notes. That sort of thing.'

'About what?' she said suspiciously. 'Not much happening at the moment to write notes about, I would have thought.'

He shrugged. 'You'd be surprised.'

'Well, come on then, surprise me by getting the coffee organised. And the tea. And some soft drinks.'

Danny leapt into action.

At first glance the room downstairs seemed to be in confusion, with everyone unpacking their painting gear and spreading it out on the tables. Megan could see more than a few disgruntled faces.

'Who could do with a hot drink now?' she called above the hubbub.

'Nowhere to put it,' the red-shirted man complained.

And that was the difficulty with the trays, of course. Megan looked round for a suitable space but couldn't find one.

Danny immediately placed his on the floor near the back wall. 'Hold yours steady,' he said.

In no time he had distributed the six mugs of coffee on Megan's, and was taking orders for tea. She picked up the other tray and held that steady too. Soon everyone had a hot drink of their choice, and Danny was handing round the plate of homemade biscuits.

'He deserves a chocolate cake all to himself for this,' Megan murmured to

Alice. 'Or even two.'

Alice smiled. 'What would we do without him?'

'There must be a catch here somewhere.'

But Alice was too busy to think about that now. 'Get him to take some to the men,' she said.

Megan snorted. 'They don't deserve it.'

'They're only doing their job.'

'And making a lot of noise about it.'

This was true, Alice thought, close to despair. Not being able to open the outside door to the garden didn't help matters either, and the day seemed to be getting darker. She drank her own coffee as soon as it was cool enough, but some of the others were taking their time over theirs, obviously discouraged.

'Let's get going again, shall we?' she called in as bright a tone of voice as she could manage.

Getting round to everyone in turn was not easy, but Alice did her best in the difficult circumstances. Eventually, though, she began to think it might be best to cut the morning short and try to placate her disgruntled group some-how . . .

⋆ ⋆ ⋆

Even when everyone had packed up and gone trailing off — jackets still wet, in spite of Megan's efforts — the room looked dreary and uninviting.

'Who would want to spend a day painting here?' Alice said.

'Or cooking.' Megan glared at the closed door to the kitchen. 'All this upheaval had better be worth it.'

Alice straightened a chair. 'Have we made the biggest mistake of our lives?'

There was a second's silence, and then they both burst out laughing.

'What's so funny?' Danny demanded, clumping down the stairs to join them, looking as if he'd attached his black notebook to his T-shirt and was holding it in place until the glue dried.

'You've got something to write about,

anyway,' Megan said, still spluttering.

'Dismal failure of *Love-in-a-Mist* Painting Workshop,' said Alice. 'Premises flooded, deafening racket at all times, freezing cold . . . '

'It's not as bad as all that,' said Danny with dignity.

'Very nearly, wouldn't you say, Megan?'

'Can we see what you've written, Danny?' Megan tried to grab his notebook.

He darted away and held it out of reach. 'It's private.'

'Everything written on these premises is our copyright,' said Megan, with a deadpan expression on her face.

He looked at her in alarm.

'Take no notice of her, Danny,' said Alice.

'Whose side are you on?' Megan demanded.

'I'm being honest, that's all.'

'And a little too generous, if you ask me,' said Megan, pointedly.

'Most of them wouldn't have come

74

back if I hadn't,' said Alice, firmly.

Danny looked from one to the other, confused. 'Hadn't what?'

Megan sighed. 'Alice has sent them home early today with the promise of another free workshop experience to make up for this disaster. She's invited this group to join with the smaller Saturday group for this week. So you'll be needed here for a repeat performance, if you can stand it.'

'And that's bad?'

Alice smiled. 'By Saturday the weather'll be better. We'll have plenty of space in here, coffee breaks on the back lawn, no hammering and racketing from the room next door, all new appliances ready for use . . . '

'And no money coming in for *Love-in-a-Mist* from the workshops this week,' said Megan in disgust. 'And there'll be no chocolate cake either, unless you're dead lucky, Danny, and find me in a good mood. I don't know what Harry's going to say.'

'Enough of this lazing about,' said

Alice. 'We'd better get started on getting all the rest of your equipment down here ready for tomorrow. Then I'll get off to the hospital and spend longer with Grandad.'

'Actually, I do know what Harry'll say,' continued Megan, half to herself. 'He'll say it's good for business. I can just see him sitting at our kitchen table, grinning at you with approval for being brave enough to make that daft suggestion. Call in at our place on your way back, why don't you, and hear what he's got to say for yourself? I might even give you a meal.'

'I take it I'm forgiven, then?'

Megan's face lit up in a smile. 'We're in this together, Alice, I know that. We need satisfied customers if we're to make anything of our new venture, even if we lose out financially.'

'Only on one more occasion, I promise.'

'We hope,' said Megan with feeling. 'We'll expect you when we see you, then. And don't be late!'

* * *

At the hospital, Alice found her grandfather leaning against his pillows and looking brighter than he had for days. There was even a little colour in his cheeks, and his eyes looked extra blue as they lit up on seeing her.

'Alice, my dear girl!'

She bent to kiss him and then pulled up the spare chair. 'You look so much better today, Grandad.'

'I think they're pleased with me, love.'

He closed his eyes for a second as if he didn't quite believe it. For a moment, she was reminded of the days after Gran died, when he had seemed to withdraw into himself in a way that had worried her. She hastened to tell him about the day's events, making light of what had happened to interest him without causing him concern.

He smiled and she let out a breath of relief.

'We've got this young boy helping us,'

she said. 'Danny. He's really good.'

'Not Freddie Crane's grandson?'

She shook her head. 'I don't think so. Danny's here on holiday, staying in a chalet somewhere.'

'Freddie's got a grandson called Danny, his daughter's boy. No, wait, I'm wrong. It's his great-grandson.'

'Danny had the coffee organised in no time for us,' Alice said. 'He's going to be a real help at my workshops. The only thing is ... ' She stopped in confusion, realising that she had almost let out something she had resolved to keep to herself. Danny's likeness to Tom Carey must surely be coincidence. And yet ... No, she wouldn't think about it.

'Freddie likes his coffee, always did. Many a time Mollie warned him that he'd be drowning in it if he wasn't careful. You're not drinking too much coffee, are you, love? Tell the boy not to make too much.'

Alice smiled and hastened to reassure him. 'The kitchen downstairs is looking good now,' she said. 'They delivered the new appliances this morning. Megan will have all that lovely space for her classes.'

'Freddie was a good friend to me in the old days,' her grandfather said, easing himself a little on the pillows. 'Worked in the mill, you know. Not the one in Lyme.'

'Oakley?'

'Oakley Mill. He's one of the family, you see. Gone to ruin now.'

'Not Freddie, I hope.'

'A good friend. Mollie liked him.'

Alice was silent for a moment, thinking of her grandmother and wishing she was still with them. But she was here to be cheerful for her grandfather's sake. For the rest of the visit, she described some of the people who had turned up this morning believing she could work wonders and turn them into successful artists immediately.

'They've all promised to come back on Saturday,' she said. 'I'm hoping we can do a bit of painting outside.' She glanced at the window, where rain was still slithering down the pane and the sky looked a deep and dismal grey.

'You've been a good girl to me, Alice,' her grandfather said rather wistfully.

'I hope I always will be, Grandad.'

He caught hold of her hand and pressed it hard as if he was extra reluctant to see her go when it was time for her to leave.

She smiled and kissed him. 'If you go on as you are doing, Grandad, you'll be joining us out there on the back lawn soon, showing what you can do.'

His answering smile seemed uncertain, but seeing him looking so much better was the best thing that had happened today. Even so, her heart was heavy as she walked out of the ward and turned in the doorway for a final wave.

5

Bright sunlight, thank goodness! Alice leapt out of bed as soon as she awoke on Saturday morning, eager to catch sight of the sun in case it vanished behind a bank of clouds as it had on the disastrous first workshop day.

She drew back her bedroom curtains and gazed out on a world that resounded with birdsong. The sky was a hazy blue. Beyond the garden, the shimmering sea looked calm and beautiful. Even Pickles' purr seemed louder today as he wound himself round her legs. She unbolted the door into the garden for him and made sure the hooks to hold it wide open were secure.

'Off you go, Pickles,' she said, bending to stroke him. 'Give me five minutes and your breakfast will be waiting for you.'

She took only minutes to shower and dress. Then she made coffee, poured cereal, and carried both down to eat on the wooden seat outside in the sunshine, enjoying the scent of damp grass and early honeysuckle that drifted across to her. After a while Pickles came to join her, purring. When he had licked his dish clean, he curled up on the paving slabs near the low stone wall edging the flower bed, where clumps of sea pinks looked like soft cushions.

Soon she would get some of the small tables and chairs set up out here so that jaded painters could come out and relax whenever they wished. Some might like to bring their easels out here and work in the fresh air. There would be no disturbances today, she hoped, and plenty of room for everyone to spread themselves out and make the most of the amenities on offer here.

A loud knocking on the door to the street surprised her, and she heard the distant bell ringing upstairs.

She rushed to unbolt the door.

'Danny!' she said, on seeing him standing there looking as if he wasn't sure of his welcome. 'How did you get here so early?'

He shrugged, and then grinned as he ran his hand through his curly hair. 'My uncle dropped me off. He had business to see to.'

'At this hour?'

'Fishing or something. He's got a boat.'

'And you didn't want to go with him?'

He glanced towards the closed door to the downstairs room now set up as a kitchen.

'I'd rather be here.'

'You must be keen.'

He shrugged. 'I can go fishing any time.'

Alice smiled as she ushered him in and bolted the door behind him. 'Go on then, take a look at our lovely new kitchen and see what you think.' She had been in to admire it several times since the fitters had left, unable to believe even now that they had done such a good job. A large stainless steel table was in the middle of the room, with plenty of space for moving around it.

Danny stood on the threshold and blinked. 'Wow!'

'You approve?' Alice said, pleased.

He ran his hand over the surface of the table. 'Cool.'

'Megan thinks so too. She can't wait to get cracking with her first group on Thursday. She'll be here shortly, and you can help her get things sorted out. She's bringing a load of stuff with her.'

'Great.'

'Care to carry some of the small tables outside first, while I get some more water in these flower jars?'

Megan had brought bunches of carnations and gypsophilla with her yesterday to decorate the window, a present from Harry. He had pointed out that, until Alice had some more paintings to display, they needed something to act as an attractive barrier between the workshop activities inside and the street outside. He was right, of course. Combined with foliage from the garden, the flowers filled five large vases and would do their job well. The scent from the carnations would also help disguise the smell of white spirit a little, she thought, as she added water to each vase. But with the windows and the door to the garden wide open today, there wouldn't be the same problem with that as there had been on Wednesday.

★　★　★

'So where are your sisters today, Danny?' Megan asked as she began to unpack the first of the huge bags she had brought with her.

'No idea.'

'They don't share your interests?'

'You could say that.'

'So what do they like doing?'

He shrugged and turned away. By the hunch of his shoulders she could see that he didn't want to be questioned. Megan knew to respect that and curb her natural curiosity. Harry had warned her often enough that it would get her into trouble one day. But that day hadn't come yet, she had pointed out each time he came out with his criticism — although she admitted she might have gone over the top once or twice. But not today. She would be like Alice, quietly interested and approachable, so that people would confide in her without her having to probe.

I wish, she thought. *I'm more likely to jump in with both feet if I'm not extra careful.* It was unusual, Danny wanting to spend his holiday helping them out. They knew so little about him really.

'I'm going to be a chef one day,' he said.

'You are? Great. So it's a good idea for you to get a bit of practice now?'

'You don't mind?'

'Mind?' Megan stopped stacking packets of sugar in one of the bottom cupboards. 'We're delighted. Apart from anything else, you were such a help on Wednesday, and will be again today when you're serving the coffee. It will leave me free to go off and collect the pans and cooking utensils when the place opens.'

Danny lifted the second bag onto the worktop for her. 'Will do. What are you teaching them first?'

'Something straightforward to start with. I need to assess their abilities, you see. Twelve have booked for the first session. *Tea for Two* is the theme. Tiny blinis to be topped with fillings of their choice, scones . . . '

'I can make scones.'

'You'd be surprised how many people can't. Cupcakes, flapjacks perhaps.'

'Sounds good.'

'I hope they think so too. Then I'll see how it goes and plan my sessions carefully. There'll be a different theme each week, and they'll find out what it is when they get here.'

'Why not before?'

'Depends on the weather and what ingredients I can get hold of. *Alfresco Lunch*, for instance. That'll be when the forecast is good so we can eat it outside and linger over it if they want.'

'Will we be eating it too?'

'Of course. You can't survive on chocolate cake alone. And you can help me judge everyone's efforts, if you like. I'll need to keep records, of course.'

He grinned. 'And mark everyone out of ten?'

'Maybe.'

'I'll like doing that.'

Megan smiled too. It would be fun having Danny working with her, she thought. He was a strange boy, but she liked him. Young as he was, there was a decency about him, a sense that he'd do his best in whatever situation he found himself.

'So where did you learn about cooking, Mrs Ross?' he asked.

'You can call me Megan. And Alice would probably rather you called her Alice. OK?'

'All right, if you want.'

'I went to Anderley Catering College. Know it? It's not far from here.'

'Think so. Was it good?'

'Excellent. But I'd be sure to say that, wouldn't I?'

'You might not if they didn't teach you much.'

'You'll have to wait and see,' Megan said, shutting the cupboard door. 'There are some more things to bring in from the car, and it's not parked very near. We'd better do it before Alice's lot arrive, or that won't suit them.'

'They'll be happier today,' said Danny.

'They'd better be,' said Megan with feeling.

* * *

Today there was a lighter atmosphere about the place as people began to arrive for the free workshop. There were no grumbles or complaints that there was too much noise coming from the

89

kitchen to disturb their concentration. As Alice had hoped, some of the group decided to set up their easels outside. While she helped the others settle themselves indoors, she could hear pleasant chat and laughter from those in the open air.

So far, so good.

There were three beginners among the people who had turned up today, and once the rest knew what they wanted to do and began to start on their work, Alice gathered the novices around her for a brief chat about choosing subjects and mixing colours. She had provided photographs of well-known scenes, animals and flowers to get people started. In addition, there was a bowl of fruit, and another of tiny objects that might prove interesting.

The morning passed pleasantly, and she had plenty of time to move among everyone and give advice and help if needed. All the time she was aware of Megan in her domain, ready to provide moral support should she need it, just as Alice would do next week when her friend was busy. Once the groups and classes had proved they were working well, this wouldn't be necessary, of course.

Danny provided hot or cold drinks after the first hour and a half. Most people downed brushes and made use of the garden.

Megan poured coffee for herself and Alice, and they stood a little way off watching everybody.

'How's it going then?' Megan asked quietly.

Alice smiled. 'Spot on. They seem pleased to be here. I think they'll be signing on, all of them.'

'I'll be ready with the booking forms and cash box to take the deposits at the end of the session for you, and . . . hello, here's someone else.'

Alice glanced at the door as a slim, neat young woman came to join them in the garden, smiling as if she expected a rapturous welcome.

'Megan Downton, you haven't changed a bit!'

Her voice was high-pitched, and her rather formal navy trouser suit looked far too hot for such a warm day. She smoothed her short blonde crop as if she was afraid a stray hair was out of place.

Megan hesitated for only a moment before stepping forward. 'Natalie Tanner! It's been a long time.'

'At least ten years,' Natalie said. 'Can you believe it?' She giggled, obviously unable to do so herself.

'I'm Megan Ross now,' Megan said.

Natalie looked incredulous. 'Don't tell me you married boring Harry?'

Alice bristled, surprised that Megan made no comment. Dear Harry, so reliable and kind. Boring, never!

'We married soon after I left college,' said Megan. 'And it's been a case of Happy Ever After ever since.'

'Kids?'

Megan's face clouded for only an instant. She shook her head. 'You?'

'I've more sense than to get tied down.' Natalie looked around her at the people beginning to make a move to get back to their easels. 'I'm meeting someone here. He's not arrived yet.'

'This isn't a public meeting place,' said Megan sharply, as Danny appeared and began collecting empty coffee mugs.

'Danny!' cried Natalie in delight.

'You know each other?'

Natalie smiled. 'You could say that, hey, Danny?'

He scowled but said nothing.

'Such a nice boy,' she said as he as he escaped indoors with his tray-load of empty mugs. 'I thought I'd just pop in and see how it's all going for old time's sake, Megan. I saw your name on the posters in the office, and so here I am.'

'The office?'

'Where I'll be working from Saturday.'

'So you're not planning to sign on for one of our groups?'

Natalie shuddered. 'Me, sign up for

slapping a bit of paint about? Not likely. And I've hardly been inside a kitchen for years, and don't intend ever doing so again.'

'So what d'you do now, then?'

'This and that. Publicity for the rest of the season. I've just landed the job at the new Tourist Team place in Cobb Alley, and we're planning a get-together for business people next Saturday evening, a week today. Like to come along? You could learn a thing or two, pick up a few tips. I'll hang around until this lot have gone and tell you more.'

'You can tell me now while Alice gets back to what she should be doing,' said Megan. 'Danny needs to be off, and you can help me with the washing-up.' She laughed at Natalie's shocked expression. 'Only joking. He'll have done it already.

'I'll get the publicity material from the car and be right back,' Natalie said.

* * *

'How did you know Danny has to get off right this minute?' Alice asked as they moved together towards the door.

'I didn't, but I know I'm right,' said Megan. 'No love lost between those two, by the look of it. One glance at her and he'll be out of the door like a bat out of hell.'

Alice smiled. 'Not much love lost between the two of you either, is there?'

'She wasn't my favourite person at college, that's for sure.'

'I gathered that much. Her remark about Harry . . . '

'Oh, that.'

'Didn't it annoy you?'

'She was after him herself once, you know. Was dead set on him.'

'D'you mean to say Harry turned her down for you?'

'Oh, he had no idea what was going on, poor man. Everyone else could see what she wanted, though.'

'He had eyes only for you?'

'I like to think so,' said Megan modestly.

Alice laughed. 'I'd better not linger out here or I'll be in trouble.'

'Miss Publicity and I will keep ourselves out of your way . . . over the other side of the lawn on that seat. That's no problem.'

'The only problem is having to spend time with her?' guessed Alice.

'All in a good cause,' said Megan.

'If you say so.'

The rest of the morning slipped by until it was time for the participants of the art workshop to sign on for the planned group sessions, if they hadn't already done so, and then to pack up and leave. Alice had shown them how the workshops would be run, and they had learnt from the delicious home-made cakes and biscuits offered at coffee time that the lunch provided at each session would be equally as good.

'Worth coming for that alone,' one elderly man joked.

Alice smiled at him as he stuffed his paints into an old shoulder-bag and heaved it up, ready to leave. He'd wrapped his brushes in newspaper, promising to clean them when he got home.

'You won't forget, Mr Winton, will you?' she said.

'Of course not, my dear. But 'Alan', please. 'A workman is only as good as his tools', certainly in my case anyway, so I intend to look after them.'

'That's the spirit.'

'But you are so much better than yours, as I saw at your open evening. So when are we going to see some more of your own excellent work?'

Before Alice could answer, there was a slight commotion as the door as Tom Carey came in, carrying a large stainless steel pedal-bin in both hands. He pushed the door shut behind him with his shoulder, and smiled at Alice in such a devastating way that for a moment she couldn't speak.

'Surplus to requirements,' he said, as he put the bin down with a clatter. 'Good idea or what? Danny said you hadn't got one.'

'*Danny!*'

'My ward.'

She rubbed one hand across her eyes, almost too tired now to take in anything much. Reaction setting in, she thought, after what could have been a tense morning.

'Why did Danny think I needed it?'

'For all the debris you'll have . . . used paper towels, old tubes of paint, newspaper that's protected your tables. That sort of thing.'

'Well, yes,' she said. 'Danny thinks of everything.'

'He's a good lad.'

A bit too good at keeping his guardian informed about what went on at *Love-in-a-Mist*, she thought. But she was being ungracious, even if he did have an ulterior motive and was using this as an excuse. 'Thanks,' she said faintly.

He nodded and then looked critically round the room.

She was only too aware of the muddle of tables and chairs, the faint hint of white spirit in the air and the blobs of blue paint on the floor by one of the easels she had provided.

'You'd better clear that up at once before someone treads it all over the place,' he said.

'All in good time,' she said stiffly.

He shot a speculative glance at her and then looked quickly away. She wanted to ask him more about Danny, and if his two sisters were also Tom's wards. But Danny had said that the girls had left after their holiday. There seemed to be some impermanence about Danny staying on too. There was an intriguing situation here. Megan would be all agog when she knew about it, wanting to know exactly what it was all about.

'So the morning was a success this time?' he said.

'Hopefully the first of many.'

'And you had a good crowd?'

Alice nodded. She wasn't going to tell him that there were still places vacant on both workshop days that she hoped would have been taken by now. He sounded truly concerned but she wasn't fooled.

'I'm glad to hear that,' he said.

She couldn't tell from his tone whether he was pleased or disappointed, but suspected it was the latter and that he was a good enough actor to pretend otherwise.

Megan and her friend were coming back across the grass now, Megan looking down and dragging her feet a little, and Natalie Tanner taking dainty steps in those high heels of hers, smiling as soon as she saw Tom.

'There you are, Tom' she said. 'I hoped you'd show up.'

Megan was gazing at him through half-closed eyes and Alice hurried to introduce them. Then she nodded unsmilingly and took a step back.

'I hope you're impressed,' she said, her tone of voice indicating that he had better be or he'd have her to deal with.

'Of course,' he said smoothly. 'A fine achievement. So far.'

Alice hid a smile as she glanced at the muddle surrounding them.

'We'd better be off,' said Natalie, beaming round at them all. 'Things to do. People to see. Isn't that right, Tom?'

He looked down at her and smiled. 'If you say so.'

Alice watched them go with a feeling of hurt that took her by surprise. He was nothing to her, except as someone she had to be wary of. Megan had no doubts as to where his interests lay, and her demeanour made it plain she wanted him off the premises.

'Let's get the clearing up done,' she said now. 'And then we'll eat out here and relax. I've made some mini pizzas I want us to try out, to go with the salad I found upstairs in your fridge. You don't mind? There's some cheese too. Then I'll show you all the details about this Tourist Evening thing Natalie left with me. Much as I dislike her, it might be a good idea for us to show up.'

'Good for publicity, anyway,' said

Alice, stretching both arms above her head.

They had straightened the tables and chairs and swept the floor before Megan noticed the shiny new bin in the corner.

'What's that?' she asked in surprise.

'A bin.'

'I can see that. But where did it come from?'

'Tom Carey brought it.'

'We could buy our own bin.'

'Just trying to be helpful.'

'It's probably a trap. Or poisoned or something. He wants us out of here fast and we mustn't forget it.'

'It was Danny's idea and he must have told Tom,' said Alice. 'He obviously had worked out that we needed a bin in here for the workshops. We were right about some sort of relationship between the two of them. Danny is Tom's ward.'

Megan stared at her in horror. 'Is he, now? And I thought Danny was our friend.' She pulled a table into a better position and slammed two chairs against it.

Alice bent to pick up some discarded newspaper and scrunched it up to throw in the bin. 'I can't believe that boy isn't keen to be here for his own sake. He's so eager to learn from you. Admit it, Megan.'

'I admit nothing. He'll have to go.'

'Please, Megan, think about it.'

'It doesn't stop him being a spy.' Megan picked up more newspaper and crushed it into a ball. She hurled it at the bin, missed, and stamped on it instead. 'That's what I'd like to do that man.'

'Why worry?' said Alice. 'We know what we've got on offer is good. All our ideas for Love-in-a-Mist are fantastic. Harry's certain that all is well with the lease. All we need is determination to succeed.'

'And we've got that in basketfuls,' said Megan, beginning to calm down.

'So we'll lighten up and enjoy the sunshine out there — and our delicious

lunch and a well-deserved rest —
before we put the finishing touches to
your arrangements for your first cookery class. Right?'

'Right,' Megan said.

She didn't sound entirely convinced,
and Alice could foresee arguments
ahead. But for the moment they could
put it to the back of their minds and
enjoy the sunshine.

And forget the way Tom Carey had
smiled at her, she thought. And how her
heart had leapt on seeing him.

6

Alice set up her easel on the far side of the lawn the following Thursday, a brand new canvas in place and her paints on a small table at her side. Her brushes were in a jar nearby, beside a container of white spirit. No danger of nasty fumes from that out here in the fresh air on this lovely morning, she thought. She felt sorry for Megan with her group of six in the warm kitchen, even though she knew her sympathy was unnecessary.

Megan, bright-eyed and confident, was in her element, and hopefully so were the members of her first class. They had looked keen as Danny greeted them at the door and handed them the cheery, checked aprons Megan had ready for them.

Alice's job was to be somewhere nearby in case she was needed. Out here working at her easel was considered the perfect place. Danny would bring her coffee at intervals, and report on the proceedings while she churned out her masterpieces.

That was Megan's idea of what should happen, anyway. Alice smiled as she squeezed paint onto her palette and searched in her box of odds and ends for her container of charcoal. How easy it sounded, but how difficult it was in practice — even with the magnificent view of Lyme Bay sparkling in front of her for inspiration.

She picked up a piece of charcoal and gazed at the coastline to the east through half-closed eyes. This morning, far-away Portland Bill was slightly hazy again, as if it preferred to keep its secrets to itself. Danny had been extra quiet on arrival this morning, she thought, slipping into the kitchen as if he preferred not to be seen either. Megan had given him a sharp look but bitten back the comments she obviously wanted to make.

Alice recalled Megan's fury when she'd learnt of the connection between the two, and how she was all for telling Danny he was no longer welcome here.

'But on what grounds?' Harry had said, when he called in on his way home from his office to pick her up.

'That's what I keep asking,' Alice had said.

'The boy's useful to you, Megan,' Harry pointed out. 'And keen to learn.'

'He'll learn too much,' she said bitterly.

'I thought you liked him.'

'I don't like the thought that he'll be passing on information.'

'About what? Your popular cookery classes? How will that help his guardian?'

'There'll be other things.'

'Like Alice's workshops?'

Megan shrugged. 'Who knows.'

'We can't tell Danny we don't want him anymore,' Alice had insisted. 'He'd be deeply hurt after all the help he's given us. As Harry says, we've nothing to hide: nothing that anyone can't see for themselves. All we have to do is work hard and get things running really well. As simple as that.'

'If you say so,' Megan had conceded reluctantly.

Alice had known that the argument would continue as soon as Megan and Harry got home, and had been relieved to learn in the end that Harry had triumphed, insisting that the boy could well be innocent of any subterfuge and they should give him the benefit of the doubt. Megan had agreed to reserve her judgement for the time being. In any case, Danny was too useful to her to risk losing his help today.

'You're going to be in my painting,' Alice told the distant headland, and then felt herself blush as she realised she had spoken out loud. It was just as well there was no one else around to hear her.

She made a charcoal mark on the canvas, then rubbed it off with a dry rag and tried again. What else had Danny

108

told his guardian about them? she wondered . . .

She finished sketching out a rough idea of what she hoped was a good composition, and stood back to look at it critically. It was hard to imagine she could make anything interesting of it, but maybe it would help to get some paint on the canvas and see if the colour helped. She picked up her brush, but the scratching sound it made as she worked wasn't as satisfying to her today as it was normally. There was too much to think about, to worry over, for her to give the art full concentration, hard as she tried.

Yesterday, Harry had talked of the popularity of her workshops, but she wasn't at all sure he was right about that. Ten people so far had paid their deposits for the ten sessions, and they would be divided between her two workshops days on Wednesdays and Saturdays. The balance of the fees would be paid weekly. It had sounded a lot of money when she had first made her plans, but now she was far from sure of that because of the expenses involved. They had already invested heavily in the tables and chairs; then there was the heating to consider, and the lunches and coffees they would provide . . .

Suppose people decided after all that this wasn't what they wanted, and stopped coming?

Alice paused and gazed at the scene in front of her. Conditions were changing out there across the bay. Clouds loomed, square-shaped, over Golden Cap, rising to the east above the edge of the sea and the highest point on the south coast. An easily recognisable beauty spot that had featured in at least two of her paintings, both of which had sold on their Open Day.

Today it was not going well.

Maybe it was because half her mind was on Megan working enthusiastically with her first group. She had promised to make extra-delicious little fairy cakes for Alice to take to her grandfather later, so he could taste for himself some of the delicacies on offer, even if his appetite had faded away these last few days.

'It will be something to show him, anyway,' she had said.

Alice had been grateful for the thought. She picked up her palette knife to make a mixture — ultramarine and burnt sienna, to create the dark shade she needed for some of the foreground — and then put it down again as Danny appeared across the lawn, carrying a mug of coffee. There was a patch of flour decorating one cheek.

'This is for you,' he said breathlessly.

'Is it going well?'

'They're all getting stuck in.' He put the mug down on the table at her side and looked at the work on her easel.

'What do you think?' she asked hopefully.

He wrinkled his nose. 'What is it?'

'Can't you see?'

'The sea's not that colour.'

'It was when I started.'

'And those don't look like trees.'

'*Trees?*'

He grinned. 'Only joking.'

'Get back inside where you belong,' she said, dipping her brush in a splodge of paint and pretending to aim it at him.

He dodged out of the way. 'It's great, Alice. Really. I wish I could paint like that.'

When he had gone, she looked again at what she had done, but knew it wasn't working well because her mind was elsewhere.

Her grandfather had drowsed for most of the time she had been with him yesterday, only opening his eyes as she bent to kiss him goodbye when it was time to leave. He had asked then for news of *Love-in-a-Mist*, anxious as always for her welfare. This evening she wanted to tell him how well things were going for them, so that he knew she was happy and fulfilled in her new life. Perhaps then his eyes would brighten a little and some colour return to his cheeks.

In theory, she had time to paint today — and she needed to do it, not only to have some canvasses to place in the window area of *Love-in-a-Mist* to act as a screen, but also to sell as a financial back-up to the business at this early stage. And if that happened, she needed to have more ready to replace them. So what was preventing her getting on with it?

Feeling frustrated, she dipped the brush in the jar of white spirit and reached for a paper towel. Then she looked at the painting in disgust. Danny was right. The sea was never this colour: not now when clouds wreathed across the sky, not earlier when she had first tripped across the grass with her painting gear. She was wasting her time, and would do better to pack up now and start again another day.

But Grandad would be disappointed in her giving up so easily.

'Stick at it, girl,' she could imagine

him saying. 'Give it time. It'll come, it'll come. As simple as that.'

But it didn't seem as if it would; and by the time Danny appeared again, with tea this time, she had had enough.

'Still going well in there?' she asked.

'Hard at it, all of them.'

'No problems?'

He shook his head. 'It's brilliant.'

'You're not just saying that?'

He looked hurt. 'I don't lie.'

'No, of course you don't,' she hastened to assure him. 'I know that. It's just that it's not going well out here.'

'Don't stay out here then. Do something else instead.'

'I hate giving up.'

'Just a change of scenery, that's all.'

She looked at him thoughtfully. 'You're wise all of a sudden.'

He looked smug. 'I'm always wise.'

She laughed. 'If you say so.'

'So what are you going to do, then?' he demanded.

She took a sip of tea. 'Thanks,

Danny. You've made me see sense. I'm wasting my time out here. There's a painting I want reframed. I'll see to it as soon as it's safe to leave Megan on her own.'

'She's not on her own,' he said. 'I'm here.'

'So you are.'

The decision made, she felt happier as she collected her paints together and screwed the top back on the jar of white spirit, to be poured down in the garden in a certain spot she had allocated. She would clean her brushes on the rickety table she had placed out of sight around the side of the building, and then she would check with Megan.

'I'm hoping to be here all the time soon,' Danny said. 'With Tom, I mean.'

'You are?'

'If Tom can manage it. He's got important plans. I hope they come off.'

'What sort of plans?'

He hesitated. 'Um, well, I don't really know.'

'I see.' She was sorry she had asked:

she should let him say anything he wanted her to know in his own good time, without any probing on her part. The words seem to hang in the air between them.

Danny scraped the toe of one trainer into a hole in the turf and looked down at it, frowning.

'Good luck, anyway,' she said, keeping her voice light. 'Since you're here, Danny, I'll take the opportunity to get off for as bit, OK?'

'OK.' He brightened. 'What shall I tell Megan?'

'That I've got business to do at Oakley Mill.'

He looked taken aback. 'What business?'

'Framing business.'

'Oh, that.'

He sounded disappointed, and she wondered what he'd had in mind for her to do instead. Danny could be a strange boy, but he was helpful, and she had no qualms about leaving him here pretending to be in charge.

'See you, then,' he called after her cheerfully as she turned to go.

* * *

Oakley Mill looked different today with the lowering clouds massed behind it. There was a strong scent of damp, crushed grass when Alice stepped out of her car, and a rising breeze stirred the quiet air. The silent waterwheel looked gloomy, as if waiting for someone to set it going.

She looked across at it with interest and saw that Tom Carey was leaning on the rails nearby and gazing at it. He wasn't aware of her at first, and only turned when she banged the car door shut after leaning inside to reach for her painting.

His face lit up with a smile as he walked across to join her. 'I wasn't expecting to see you here.'

'I've business to attend to with the framer,' she said.

'Martin's somewhere about.'

'I know. I phoned to check he was here.'

Tom eyed the wrapped painting Alice held closely to her. 'A new one?'

'Hardly. The paint wouldn't have dried yet.'

'There is that.' He smiled as if he knew exactly what she had brought.

For a moment she hesitated, reluctant to move towards Martin's workshop and admit her mistake. But it had to be done. The geese were absent today, but she heard the distant quack of a duck and then a splash as it went into the pond.

Martin looked up as she went in and stopped what he was doing at the back of the workshop among the piles of wooden battens. He smiled and came towards her. 'We meet again.'

Alice placed her painting on the counter and pulled off the wrapping. 'I don't like how it looks after all,' she said. 'It's my fault, I know. I'd like you to reframe it for me, if you would.'

Martin looked at it for a moment in

silence and then reached for his rack of samples. He extracted one and held it against the painting for her to see how it looked. 'What do you think about this one?'

Even now she wasn't sure.

'Shall I take it out of the frame to make it easier?' he said.

With the darker frame removed, she could see at once that this was the one. The light wood drew out colours in the painting she had hardly known were there, and improved the whole thing.

'It's perfect,' she said.

He flicked open his measuring tape, jotted down a few numbers on a scrap of paper and then consulted his list of prices.

'When can I collect it?' she asked.

Martin frowned. 'Let's see . . . '

'In about half an hour?' said a voice behind her.

She spun round. She might have known that Tom couldn't keep away. 'No, it's all right,' she said. 'I can come back.'

'It's just about possible to do it while she waits, isn't it, Martin?'

'Since I owe you one, Tom.'

Tom smiled. 'Fair enough. And while you're at it, I'll borrow your kettle and a couple of folding chairs.'

Alice was outside before she knew it, annoyed with herself for allowing him to take over. But she had to admit that having the reframed painting to take back with her would be useful. She took a deep breath and tried to relax.

A sudden burst of sunshine lit up the weathered stone of the mill building and brightened the dull water in the millpond. She walked towards it and leaned on the railings as Tom had done earlier, mesmerised by the movement of the water down below in the shimmering breeze.

'Great, isn't it?' Tom said. With a flick of his wrist he unfolded first one chair and then the other. 'Here, take a seat. I'll be right back.'

He had placed them in a good position on a smooth patch of grass. As she seated herself, she heard the cluck and murmur of hens somewhere out of sight, and then the duck again. In the distance a dog barked. It occurred to her that she hadn't seen Pickles since giving him his breakfast this morning. Maybe he'd tried his luck in the kitchen with Megan, waiting for titbits. But poor disgruntled Pickles would have been turned out immediately if so, and would then have gone off, offended, on some pursuit of his own. She would make a fuss of him when she got back to show he was still loved.

She was smiling when Tom came back carrying a tray of tea things.

'Something amusing you?' he said.

'No geese about today?'

He placed the tray on the ground between them. 'I saw them in the field beyond the pond over there earlier,' he said.

'They make good watchdogs.'

'Too good sometimes. They took a particular dislike to one poor chap and wouldn't let him get anywhere near the place. Luckily I was on hand to rescue him. Martin likes to have some livestock about the place. He's got an old lean-to out at the back and they put themselves to bed at night.'

'Safe from foxes?'

'The chap in the cottage down the lane shuts them up at night and lets them out in the mornings. The hens are his.'

He bent to pour out the tea and she saw that there was a smudge of grease on the back of his neck, half-hidden by his navy jersey.

'Sugar?'

'No thanks.' She took the cup from him. 'So how did Martin come to have a framing business out here in this derelict place?'

Tom frowned. 'He needed somewhere urgently and he was glad to rent it. But the place wasn't always the mess it's in today.'

Now she had offended him. 'It's beautiful just like as it is,' she said. 'I can see that. But once it was a working mill. Now it's just ruins. It must be very old.'

'Late seventeenth century.'

She was silenced by the deep feeling in his voice. This place mattered to him and she had touched a nerve.

He took a gulp of tea. 'My family owned it. Or still own it, I should say. My grandfather was the miller here, employed by his uncle. It's complicated.'

'I see,' she said, but of course she didn't. She thought of her grandfather saying that Danny was the great-grandson of his old friend, Freddie Crane, who worked here. Or who *had* worked here. He must have died some years ago, from what she could make out, even though Grandad appeared to think otherwise. So what relation would that make him to Tom?

It was on the tip of her tongue to ask why he hadn't set up a showroom for his own work where Martin was now. But then, who would come all the way out here to a derelict site just to browse around? Martin's business was quite a different matter, of course; he provided a necessary service for the many artists in the area, which made coming out here worth their while.

Tom gazed at the silent millwheel. 'I want more than anything to get that going again. As long ago as I can remember, I've wanted that. It's what interested me in engineering in the first place.'

'And what sort of mill was it?'

'It was a grist mill.'

'For grinding corn?'

'Barley, mainly. The wheel is constructed from cast-iron hubs and side plates, with sheet metal buckets supported on a solid oak staff. Most of the sheet metal has rusted away now. It would be a huge job to renovate it.'

'And expensive.'

'That too. The place was farmed as well, of course, but the mill was the main source of income for the family for generations, until mechanisation took over in a big way and huge factories for the milling of grain were built. Progress, you see.'

She gazed up at the wheel and felt a stir of sympathy for him. 'And this is all part of our heritage.'

He smiled sadly.

'Your grandparents lived here?'

'My father too, while he worked the farm. Before he met my mother. She was from the States, over here on some teaching scheme. She never settled here, so the farm was sold, and they moved away to a place in Surrey where he became farm manager to Lord Bickley for a while.'

'And you were born there?'

He nodded as he reached for his cup, took a sip and put it down again. 'I was sent away to school in Lincolnshire at an early age, and when my mother died I used to spend most of the holidays here with my great-uncle.'

He was silent after that. She was, too, as she reflected on how Tom must have thought of this place as home. And now it was in ruins, uncared-for by this great-uncle he mentioned. Dead too, perhaps? Why didn't he try to make something of it, or at least put it on the market? Someone, surely, would see the potential.

'Complicated,' she said quietly.

'Indeed.'

The silence between them after that felt companionable, and Alice was content to sit there listening to the rustling water. There was a distant quack, and some hissing that got louder as the flock of geese appeared round the corner of the house. They seemed to look round in surprise to see two people sitting on chairs that hadn't been there before. One of the geese hissed louder, head down, then gave up and wandered away with his friends to look for someone to attack.

'Are they really as fierce as they seem?' Alice asked.

'They're usually no harm unless someone upsets them. More tea?'

She shook her head. 'It must be nearly time to collect the painting.'

He drained his cup. 'We'll go and see.'

She felt strangely reluctant to move but it had to be done. Tom got up too. 'I'll clear this lot away in a minute.'

She'd hoped he would do it now, but she could hardly refuse to walk to Martin's workshop with him.

Martin had just finished and looked up, smiling, as she went in. 'So, here we are, my dear.' He held up the framed painting for Alice to see.

She exclaimed in delight. 'What a difference the frame makes!' Then she caught a conspiratorial look between the two men.

'You made a good choice, Tom,' Martin said.

She froze. Earlier, Martin had shown her one example only. She had agreed at once, not realising that Tom probably had a pact with him to push this one forward without giving her the chance to see more. It was true she liked it because it set the painting off to perfection, and it would most likely have been her choice anyway, but that wasn't the point.

She paid what she owed, and waited while Martin produced his roll of bubble wrap and sticky tape. When he had finished wrapping the painting, Tom stepped forward to pick it up. This time Alice was too quick for him. She grabbed it and marched out into the sunshine, across the yard to where her car stood waiting.

'Wait a minute!' With his longer legs, Tom caught up with her before she reached her vehicle. 'I was only trying to help,' he said.

She spun round. 'By interfering?'

'That wasn't my intention.'

'It seems very like it to me.'

'I've annoyed you.' For a moment he looked cast down, as if he was genuinely hurt at her reaction.

'I don't like you standing by all the time, waiting for me to fail,' she said.

He smiled suddenly and quirked one eyebrow. 'You think you can manage to do that on your own?'

She let out an exclamation of annoyance and opened the car door. Only afterwards as she drove over the bridge and headed for the lane did she wonder if she had made a big mistake here. What possible harm could he do by suggesting the best option? Even so, she would do well not to trust him too much.

She glanced in the rear mirror. He was no longer standing there watching her but stacking the folding chairs against the railings. As he stooped to pick up the tea tray, his shoulders looked strangely vulnerable. She wondered if he still had that grease mark on the back of his neck.

7

'You have wheelchair access, of course?'

Amidst the chattering noise of a hundred people crammed into the Function Room of the Belle View Hotel, Alice had to strain hard to hear what Natalie Tanner was saying.

'Wheelchair access?' she said.

'At *Love-in-a-Mist*.'

Alice thought of the trouble the men had had, manoeuvring the kitchen appliances in the other day — but that was only because of the tables that restricted their path. She smiled.

'Of course.'

Natalie nodded her sleek head. 'Tom said you had, but I needed to make sure, so I'm glad you're here this evening.'

She seemed so officious, standing there in her neat black suit and high heels, that Alice felt the same unease as she had when meeting her the other day. Natalie wasn't an inspector checking up on them, so why did she sound like one? She even had a notebook in one hand. She opened it now and frowned at something she saw written there. If someone else had asked her the same question, Alice thought, she would have considered it reasonable from a member of the newly-set-up Tourist Team, but Natalie merely irritated her. She was being unfair.

'That's all right, then,' Natalie said as she consulted her notes. 'I see you have an art tutor booked for next Saturday.'

'I hope that's allowed?'

Natalie nodded. 'You've already met him?'

'Should I have?'

'Then you don't know his requirements?'

Requirements? This was getting ridiculous. Alice looked round for Megan and Harry but couldn't see them in the throng. She turned back to Natalie, but she was talking to someone else now, no doubt asking their mother's maiden name to write in her little green book.

'Why so serious?' Tom's deep voice at her side made her start.

'Because it's a serious occasion.'

'You think so?'

'Natalie certainly does.'

'She's just doing her job.'

'I suppose so,' Alice acknowledged.

It was on the tip of her tongue to ask if there was anything about next Saturday's tutor, Torville Satterly, that she ought to know; but she thought better of it. She had booked him through a reputable agency, and he had sounded friendly on the phone. He had suggested she consult his website, and she'd been impressed when she got it up on her laptop screen. Her list of bookings had soon been full.

Tom quirked one eyebrow at her. 'Torville Satterly?'

'What about him?'

'You've booked him for a workshop?'

'What if I have?'

'You should think again.'

Alice was indignant. 'For what reason?'

He hesitated.

Before he could speak, she said, 'This is my business, not yours. Please keep out of our affairs.'

He gave her a look she couldn't fathom. 'I'm supposed to be doing my job of urging everyone into the next room for the cheese and wine,' he said.

'Then that's where I'll find my friends,' she said.

The glitter in his eye was unnerving.

'Is something else wrong?' she asked.

'Very much all right. There's a question-and-answer session in here afterwards, which should prove interesting.'

He looked as if he knew something was brewing, and she had a moment's suspicion that it involved *Love-in-a-Mist* in some way they hadn't thought of. But she must appear confident that all was well there. She smiled — and then hastened to find Megan and Harry in the other room.

Harry, smart in his navy jacket and chinos, was standing near the seated Meg, with a glass in one hand and a cheese straw in the other.

Megan waved to her, looking pale. 'What a scrum in there. I couldn't stand it any longer. We escaped as soon as we could.'

'I was talking to Natalie,' Alice said.

'Then you need a drink.'

'And Tom after that.'

'Two drinks.'

'You're not having anything, Megan?' Alice asked.

'A sandwich, that's all.'

'The food's good,' said Harry, helping himself to a sausage roll from the table and then a cheese and tomato sandwich.

'He's building his strength up for the gig racing at Portland tomorrow,' said Meg. 'You'll come with us and keep me company while he's proving his worth, won't you, Alice? It won't be a wasted day. There's plenty of scope for your paintbrush there.'

'Charcoal and sketchbook, perhaps.'

'You're up for it?'

'Definitely.'

This room was filling up now, and the three of them were among first to return to the Function Room, where rows of seats facing the stage had been placed ready.

They sat down in the back row.

'Useful for a quick getaway if it gets boring,' Megan muttered.

Alice smiled. 'You think of everything.'

At first the questions were about publicity for the various locations and planned events in the town, with some useful names and telephone numbers that Alice jotted down on the pad she had brought with her. Natalie and the rest of the team dealt with everything efficiently, and when Tom raised his hand she smiled at him with encouragement.

He stood up, and a frisson of interest ran through the room.

'I have a question about leases on

properties,' he said, in his deep voice that, in spite of herself, set Alice's pulses racing. 'Should a verbal promise, given in good faith but without witnesses, be honoured?'

She heard Megan move uneasily in her seat.

'He's wasting his time,' said Harry from the other side of her.

A few rows in front of them, Tom squared his shoulders, as if he was preparing for a fight and would give no quarter.

Natalie smiled. 'I understand this is a serious problem. Our legal expert was unable to be here this evening, but I've already put it to him and taken his advice. But someone here may also be able to help.' She looked enquiringly towards the others at the table with her.

The deep silence in the room seemed deafening to Alice, and yet she had no reason for alarm. She trusted Harry implicitly. All the same, Tom's voice held such assurance he sounded convincing.

The other three at table shook their heads and a murmur passed between them. Obviously Tom had made his position clear to most of them already.

'I think we should go,' said Megan quietly.

But before they could stand up, Natalie raised her hand. 'We shall continue to look into the matter, Tom, of course, but in the meantime I know of another property that might suit your purposes if you are interested?' She looked expectantly at him, her head held a little to one side.

'What about the old warehouse near the boatyard?' someone else said.

'That's going to be knocked down.'

'No good, then.'

'There's Jones's old place.'

'He's already let it to that chap from Yeovil.'

Natalie picked up the bell from the table and rang it vigorously.

There was another silence, and she let this one last for at least a minute. She glanced round the room as if checking for spies.

'We can discuss this further in private after the meeting if you wish, Mr Carey,' she said at last, her eyes bright.

Tom obviously agreed with that suggestion because he sat down again. Alice saw that from the back he looked totally relaxed.

'Right then,' said Harry, getting up. 'Had enough? It seems that the proceedings are about to wind up.'

They followed him outside into air that smelt of seaweed. Alice took a deep breath, relieved to be out of the busy hall.

Harry had parked his car in the space Megan used when she came to *Love-in-a-Mist*, and as they walked up the hill towards it he smiled in satisfaction.

'You're looking smug, Harry,' Megan accused, puffing a little.

'Content, that's all,' he said.

'Then tell us the good news, why don't you?'

'You haven't worked that out for yourselves?'

Alice hadn't been able to think of anything but Natalie's complacent expression when Tom agreed to talk things over with her after the meeting. They'd probably go to somewhere far more exotic than the building they had just left, with its high ceilings and bare walls that gave the impression no one loved it.

'If Tom Carey gets fixed up with alternative accommodation for his showroom, he'll be off your backs,' said Harry.

Megan brightened. 'I hadn't thought of that. That's brilliant, isn't it, Alice?'

Alice nodded, surprised by her feeling of dismay. There was a certain satisfaction in striving to get *Love-in-a-Mist* up and running in spite of his attempts to jeopardise their efforts. She would miss that.

Megan laughed. 'No more of him hanging round *Love-in-a-Mist* watching our every move, or showing up every time you visit Oakley Mill. Danny, all is forgiven!'

'Fancy a coffee or something?' Alice said as they reached the car.

Harry yawned. 'Best get back, but thanks anyway. Another time, perhaps. We've got an early start tomorrow, all of us. You're coming too, aren't you, Alice; to keep this wife of mine under control while I do the gig racing?'

* * *

Alice had never actually witnessed a gig race before, and was surprised at the amount of equipment Harry was placing in his car when she arrived at Rose Lodge early on Sunday morning.

'Surely you're not planning to get the boat in there as well?' she said.

But Harry didn't laugh. 'Megan's not well.' His voice was flat and he looked paler than usual. 'Go on in, Alice. She'll be pleased to see you.'

She found Megan in the large, rambling kitchen at the back of the house, seated on the old leather sofa that was so comfortable, Harry had refused to get rid of it when they bought a sparkling new one. And so it had landed up here, and looked right at home with the copper pans hanging from the beams and the rag rug in front of the Aga.

Megan smiled when she saw Alice, but was definitely not her normal exuberant self as she lay back on the sofa. 'Harry's fussing for nothing,' she said. 'I ate something that disagreed with me, that's all. I'll be all right in a bit.' She took a sip from the glass of water on the table nearby.

'You don't look all right,' Alice said as she sat down beside her.

'Thanks for the compliment.'

'You're not still thinking of going today if you're ill? Be sensible, Megan.'

'When am I ever sensible?'

'You have a point there.'

'You're supposed to argue with me.'

'But you're too ill to argue. It might send your blood pressure up.'

'I haven't got blood pressure,' said Megan indignantly.

Harry came in then. 'I've got to go,' he said. He hesitated. 'I'm the cox, you see and it's a bit late to . . .'

'Please don't worry,' said Alice. 'I'll be here with Megan until I'm sure she feels better. We can both come on afterwards in my car. I'll need to come home before the rest of you anyway, so I can get to the hospital in good time this evening.'

'If you're sure,' Harry said doubt-fully.

'Hey,' said Megan, indignantly. 'I'm here too, you know.'

'She sounds better already,' said Alice. 'Go on, Harry, or you'll be late.'

He bent to kiss his wife, waved his thanks to Alice and was off.

'You do want to go today, Megan, don't you?' Alice said.

Megan didn't answer and Alice looked at her reproachfully. 'You're not ill at all,' she accused. 'You've deceived Harry.'

'He'd be so disappointed if he knew watching gig racing bores me stiff,'

Megan said. 'I knew you wouldn't mind, you see, Alice. We can go down to the harbour in Lyme instead, so you can paint. What's the difference?'

A lot, Alice thought. She had been looking forward to a restful time away from Lyme, with no danger of another confrontation with Tom when she was least expecting it. But that was selfish, and why would it matter to her in the slightest now?

'Surely Harry will worry about you if we don't show up, Megan,' she said.

Megan pulled her mobile phone out of her pocket with a flourish. 'See this? I'll give him time to get to Portland and then use it. I'll tell him I'm more or less OK now, but we've decided to stick to Lyme, just in case, and to give you plenty of time to visit the hospital. He won't mind.'

'You're the limit,' said Alice.

'But he loves me.'

'And you don't think he would if you told him that gig racing doesn't interest you? I'm sure that's not true. He's too good a man to be messed about.'

'It's for his own good.'

'What a stupid phrase that is,' said Alice crossly.

Megan sprang up. 'We're wasting time. You could be down at the harbour at this very minute, churning out masterpieces. What are we waiting for?'

They drove in Alice's car and parked in her usual place. Since they weren't going by car to Portland after all, she took the opportunity to collect her oil paints and everything else she needed, including her easel.

From there it was a short walk down the hill to the seafront and along to the harbour, where boats bobbed at their moorings and children played on the sandy beach nearby. She chose a place on the Cobb that gave shelter from the westerly breeze and started to unpack her painting gear.

Megan went off to investigate acquiring some coffee to bring back, and to phone Harry. She was gone such a long time that Alice had sketched the scene in front of her and placed the canvas on her easel ready to begin. For a while, she studied the view she had chosen, working out the best focal point and noticing how the cottages further along fitted in to their surroundings as if they had always been there. She chose the tubes of paint she would need and squirted some of each onto her palette. The sun was fitful today, but the shadows from the clouds made interesting patterns on the water.

At last Megan returned, looking flushed and carrying two polystyrene cups of coffee. 'Here,' she said, handing one to Alice. 'I had to go a long way. I ran all the way back.'

She pulled the top off her own as she seated herself on the low stone ridge behind them. 'Guess who I saw?'

'I simply can't.'

'Tom Carey. Danny was with him.'

'Nothing remarkable in that.'

'Only they were carrying a ladder between them, one at either end, and Natalie Tanner was in the middle wearing shorts and a skimpy top.'

But Alice didn't want to think about that. She picked up a palette knife to mix some cerulean blue with white, to get the shade she needed for the sky.

'They looked as if they knew where they were going,' said Megan. 'They seemed like a real family on holiday, the three of them, except for the ladder. You don't take a ladder on holiday.'

When Alice didn't answer, Megan took a sip of her coffee, gazed for a moment at a boat being made ready to go out to sea, and then said: 'I followed them. Don't you want to know where they went?'

By a great effort of will, Alice shook her head. 'It can't matter to us as long as he keeps away from *Love-in-a-Mist*.'

'It surprised me, I must say. I didn't even know that little boatyard was there — tucked away at the edge of town, right against the cliff.'

'No wonder you were a long time.'

'They didn't see me.'

'I should hope not.'

'Don't let your coffee get cold, Alice. And stop painting so fast. You look as if you're desperate to win a race.'

'It *is* a race,' said Alice. 'A race against time. It'll all look so different when the tide's out and it's not hanging about.'

'Well, yes, I can see that.' Megan drank the rest of her own coffee, crumpled the cup and looked round for a bin.

'Can you see the way the light is shining now on that arm of the harbour wall?' said Alice. 'I've got to be quick or I won't catch how it is now.'

'Don't mind me,' said Megan. 'I'll wander off for a bit.'

For a while Alice worked hard, totally absorbed and inspired by the colourful scene in front of her. She was only vaguely conscious of the comments made by passers-by as they paused to watch what she was doing.

Then, drained, she put down her brush and looked around. There was no sign of Megan, which wasn't surprising if she had wandered into the narrow shopping street that couldn't be seen from here. How selfish she had been, deciding to bring her paints and getting stuck in straight away. Sketching at Portland was one thing, but once she started painting it was hard to think of anything else. She would make it up to Megan this afternoon and finish her painting later.

At last, Alice stood back from her easel to look at her work critically. This was always a good moment if it had been going well, because she often surprised herself. And today she was pleased.

Another boat was going out from the harbour, easing its way among the moored craft. She watched as it moved slowly past and saw that in it were three people. Tom, at the tiller, was wearing a navy jersey, and Natalie had on an orange life jacket and was clinging to the side as if she thought he would tip them over. Danny, obviously enjoying himself, was in the bows. The only wonder was that Megan wasn't in there too, interrogating them, Alice thought with a smile. Then she saw her friend returning along the quay carrying a package that smelt decidedly interesting.

'Did you see that?' Megan demanded.

'It's allowed,' Alice said.

'I'd like to know where they're going.'

'It's a wonder you didn't ask.'

'I've only just noticed them.' Megan threw down the parcel and climbed up the steps to stand on the top of the Cobb. 'I'm going further along,' she called down. 'I need to get a better view.'

She was soon back. 'I can't see them,' she said breathlessly. 'They must have gone to shore somewhere on Western Beach. There are cottages along there.'

'And good luck to them.'

Megan flopped down on the bottom step. 'Just you wait, Alice. I don't trust him an inch.'

Alice wiped her brushes and dipped

them into her jar of white spirit. Then she wiped them again.

'What have you been buying, Megan?' she asked, to distract her.

'Ah, yes. Bacon butties from that place along there. I couldn't resist. I don't know about you but I'm starving.'

The rolls she unwrapped were huge, thick with bacon, and Alice looked at hers in dismay. Her appetite seemed to have vanished now. She wondered where Tom and Natalie were lunching. Maybe they'd taken food with them. They could have anchored somewhere, and . . .

'Something wrong with yours?' asked Megan.

Alice took an experimental bite, and the rush of hot bacon smell made her eyes water.

'Thanks, Megan. It's great.'

'We could hire a boat,' said Megan.

'Oh, *please*!' said Alice. 'Let it drop. I've forgotten about seeing them already.' *If only that were true*, she thought.

Megan finished eating and wiped her mouth with the back of her hand. She gave a sigh of pleasure. 'Another coffee?'

'I'll get them,' said Alice. 'I could do with a walk. Don't touch anything while I'm away, Megan.'

She took the rest of her roll with her and fed it to a starving seagull. Not a good thing to do, since it was antisocial to encourage them in their greedy ways, but today she simply didn't care. Anyway, she felt sorry for it, perched there on a post away from its friends, who were doing a bit of scavenging on the other side of the harbour where a group of teenagers were eating pasties.

She strolled along, taking in the busy scene and making a mental note of anything that might make a good picture for another day. Maybe one morning she could come with her group to sketch down here. It would be a good experience for those who had never done it before.

She wondered what Tom and Natalie

151

were doing now, and where they were. Danny would probably tell her if he called in tomorrow. He had seemed to be enjoying himself, anyway, and that was good.

Hang on to that thought, she told herself.

8

Torville Satterly, the art tutor Alice had booked for the following Saturday, turned out to be overweight and bearded. He bounded in, clutching a holdall and a folded easel.

'Torville Satterly?' said Alice, coming forward with a smile.

He dropped his cargo to the floor with a clatter. 'And you must be Alice, sweet Alice,' he boomed. 'Delighted to meet you.' He held her hand in a tight grip just a few seconds too long.

He was early, and that was good, but Alice wasn't too sure of his approach. He had been booked to talk to them about flower painting and demonstrate some of his own delicate pastel work, but his fingers looked like bunches of bananas and his exuberant personality filled the room in such a way she couldn't imagine anything dainty holding the least interest for him. Flower petals would crumble and leaves wither at his glance.

'Coffee?' she said in sudden inspiration. 'Please take a seat and some will soon be organised.'

He saw her glance at his belongings. 'I'll move them out of the way. I brought my easel. Is that your work in the window?'

Alice smiled and edged towards the kitchen. 'I normally paint in oils. I'm looking forward to trying another medium.'

'Me too,' he said.

She was surprised. 'You're not familiar with pastels?'

His eyes gleamed. 'Does that worry you?'

'A bit,' said Alice. 'But of course you won't receive a fee if you don't come up with the goods.'

He gave a deep rumbling laugh that shook his whole body. 'Ha, thought I'd caught you but you're too smart for me!'

And too trusting, she thought, wishing she had arranged a meeting with him before making a booking. He might easily swamp some of the more timid members of her groups and put them off completely. But perhaps he would calm down a little during this next hour before the planned start time. He would have some preparation to do, and while he was busy she could drop a hint that there were would be several beginners here today who needed careful handling. And others, too, who wouldn't like booming voices and the floor shaking every time he stomped around.

As she had thought, Megan, in the kitchen, was fully aware that Torville Satterly had arrived, and already had the kettle on.

'He looks as if he'll do full justice to my lunch,' she said, grinning. 'Second helpings, definitely; maybe thirds. Just look at the size of him!'

'You've seen him?'

'That's what cracks in the door are

for — to peer through!' said Megan. 'You're in for a good time, my friend, I can see.'

Alice frowned. 'We could be in for trouble.'

'We can deal with him between us,' Megan said with confidence. 'Torville Satterly . . . what a name!'

'He can't help that.'

'He could change it.'

'Why should he?'

'His mother probably chose John for him,' said Megan as she poured coffee into three mugs and put two on a tray with a jug of milk and a bowl of sugar lumps. 'I expect she took one look at him at birth and thought of something more exotic at once.'

'You're being crazy.'

'But it's cheered you up.'

Alice smiled as she picked up the tray, and with her came Megan, anxious to make Torville Satterly's acquaintance.

'I'm Megan, the cook for the day,' she said.

He grinned at her. 'Another beauty! My luck's in. I hope you're well-qualified to look after the inner man?'

While I have to cope with the outer one, Alice thought, as she handed him coffee.

'Two years at catering college,' Megan said smartly. 'A fabulous job in a local restaurant for a few years until I married. Since then, occasional catering for large functions round and about the place. Will that do?'

He wrinkled his nose. 'For a start. What's on the menu today? Will you show me your kitchen?'

Megan looked pleased. 'Why not?'

They seemed to be getting on well, Alice thought, as she sipped her coffee. The breathing space this gave her was welcome, but as time went on she began to wonder how long they would be closeted in the other room, and if Harry had anything to worry about.

She could see it was likely to be a stressful day.

Torville had made it clear he would provide the materials for the pastel work and they would be working on flat surfaces. She had rearranged the tables because easel space would not be needed. Everything was ready. Alice surveyed the room with pleasure and then opened the door into the garden. Pickles came sidling in, looked round in surprise, and then jumped, purring, onto the windowsill.

Idly, Alice stroked his soft fur, wondering if anyone minded if he stayed there. She would have to ask. Outside, the shadows flickered on the grass and in the distance the sea was shimmering blue in the sunshine. Danny would be here soon and would make himself useful setting out the chairs and small tables on the grass, ready for later on. She wondered if he would still be full of the boat ride he'd enjoyed on Sunday. Maybe they had called in at the boatyard for the picnic basket Tom had ordered, and then set off down the coast as far as Beer.

It was possible. Anything was possible in her imagination, even if it pained her to think about it. But this was crazy. She had worries enough already, without adding to them.

The outside door opened and Danny came in with a rush. 'Is he here?'

Alice nodded towards the closed kitchen door. 'Can't you hear him in there talking to Megan?'

His eyes widened. 'That's good. Natalie said he wouldn't show up.'

'Oh?'

'She said he liked annoying people by letting them down.'

'And you believed her?'

'Why not? Tom does.'

'Ah yes, Tom. So you know what Tom thinks, do you?'

'I live with him, don't I?' said Danny indignantly.

'We didn't ask your surname,' said Alice.

'Colville. I'm Daniel Montgomery

Colville. A good name, don't you think? But what's that got to do with anything?'

She shrugged. 'And you're not on holiday?'

'We were at first. The girls went back, but I stayed on. That's the way Tom wants it, and his housekeeper doesn't mind if I stick around. It's only supposed to be temporary, but I might be starting at school here next week.'

The kitchen door burst open and Torville emerged, red-faced.

Alice looked at him in alarm.

'She threw me out. I was merely giving her some advice,' he said, enraged. Catching sight of Pickles, he shuddered. 'A black cat!' he said with horror. 'You'll be producing a broomstick next.'

'I could get you one,' Danny offered, looking interested.

'Not likely.'

This had gone far enough. 'Pickles can go outside,' Alice said. 'I'll see he doesn't bother you.'

Torville blinked, yanked a large handkerchief from the pocket of his jeans and wiped his eyes. 'Allergic to cats,' he said apologetically.

People were beginning to arrive now, and by the time Alice had shooed a reluctant Pickles out and come back again, Torville had emptied his holdall of boxes of pastels and sheets of paper. His easel was in position in the front, and on it was a sheet of pastel paper attached to a board.

So far, the morning had started in an unorthodox way, and Alice had had no time to feel nervous. The atmosphere was decidedly relaxed as she introduced their tutor for the day.

'Call me Torville,' he said, beaming round at them all.

So far, so good.

By lunchtime, Alice was exhausted, but she couldn't think why. Along with the rest of the group, she had enjoyed Torville's demonstration, interspersed with jokes about former students of his whom, if he could be believed, were a crowd of ignorant dolts who did everything wrong and made his life a misery. She wondered what he would be saying about them to future groups.

Megan's lunch, served buffet-style out in the garden, was a great success. Torville, his mouth full, was as entertaining as he had been earlier. Looking round at them all, Alice was pleased to see everyone enjoying themselves. She hoped they would be as pleased with what they had produced today as they were with the tutor.

★　★　★

The last of the evening sun caught the brass door handle on her grandfather's cottage, illuminating it like a beacon as Alice walked along the seafront towards it. By the time she reached it, the sunlight had dimmed, and she smiled as she inserted the key in the lock and pushed the door open. The inside smelt slightly musty, and there was a cobweb decorating the umbrella stand in the narrow passage; she made a mental note to deal with that before she left.

She went into the crowded front room, dimmed by the fading light and the dark furnishings, and switched on the light. The photographs on the mantelpiece were still there in their old-fashioned frames, just as Gran had arranged them.

Yes, there they were: Grandad and his friend Freddie Crane, smart in best suits and short haircuts, looking proudly back at whoever was taking the photograph. Alice picked it up to look at closely. A long-ago scene frozen in time, she thought; so nostalgic and sad. But the photograph itself wasn't sad. There they were, two handsome young men, about to go off somewhere special by the look of them. It was easy to imagine the light in her grandfather's eyes at the thought of good times ahead. Even during her visit to the hospital today, there had been brief twinkles in those blue eyes of his as he talked of his best friend and the good times they had enjoyed together, when they were young and had their lives in front of them. Freddie had died many years ago, but to her grandfather it was as if it were yesterday.

'Will you find that photo of us both, Alice my dear?' he had asked, clutching her hand as she bent to kiss him.

'Of course,' she promised. 'I'll go straight to the cottage now and I'll bring it with me when I come tomorrow.'

'So kind,' he murmured. 'You've been a good girl to me, Alice. And to Gran too.'

She had smiled as she left, knowing this small thing she could do really meant something to him.

Now, looking at the photograph, she saw that Freddie Crane's hair was thick and wavy. Had he grown it longer, it would probably have been as curly as young Danny's, his great-grandson. But she wouldn't dwell on that — or on the image of Tom's similar hair, either.

Instead, she found a soft cloth in a

kitchen drawer and wrapped the photograph carefully to carry back to her flat, ready to be taken to the hospital tomorrow. That done, she checked the two small bedrooms and the bathroom, and ran lightly back down to the hall. A quick look in the kitchen to make sure all was well and she was ready to go.

The sun had vanished now, leaving a ribbon of pale orange on the horizon. After locking the cottage door behind her she stood for a moment, gazing out over the harbour where a few boats lay still at their moorings in the quiet of the evening. It was a beautiful scene and one which Grandad had never tired of. She wished he could see it now, in the last of the light stealing across the water, with the ripples from the incoming tide. She couldn't bear to tear herself away, so she crossed over to the edge of the esplanade and stood resting her arms on the railings with the photograph at her feet, letting the peace of the evening steal over her.

She was hardly conscious of the few

passers-by until one of them stopped near her and cleared his throat. She knew it was Tom, even before she turned to look and saw him standing there in the suit and tie he'd been wearing at the Tourist Team Evening.

'All alone?' he asked.

She nodded, aware that she was trembling, but not being able to do anything about it.

'And you?'

He looked at her closely. 'That tutor you booked . . . he's not been harassing you?'

She looked at him for a moment in silence. 'Torville Satterly?' she said at last. 'Why should you think that?'

'You seem upset.'

'But not by Torville Satterly.'

'You're quite sure?'

'Oh, for goodness' sake!' she cried.

'He has a bad reputation.'

'I'm well able to look after myself.'

He frowned. 'But there *is* something wrong, isn't there?'

His concern seemed genuine but she

was afraid to believe it. To her horror, tears welled in her eyes. She swallowed hard. 'My grandfather . . . '

'He's taken a turn for the worse?'

'No . . . I . . . ' She let out a gasp and turned her face away so that he shouldn't see her tears. 'Please . . . '

'I'm truly sorry,' he murmured. 'I know how ill your grandfather is, and how fond you are of him.'

'He's so alone, so ill. I wish I could do more to help him.'

'Being there for him must help him. Knowing you're near, Alice.'

She sighed. 'I feel so helpless.'

'It's getting late. Have you eaten? We can go and find somewhere now, if you like?'

She shook her head. 'I . . . I can't. I'm not hungry.'

He was silent for a moment, but obviously accepted her decision because he didn't press it. He bent to pick up the photograph in its soft covering and held it out to her, disturbing the cloth just a little so that the corner of the frame showed.

'It's a photograph,' she said, taking it from him and pulling the cloth further aside to show him. 'My grandfather as a young man.'

'I know this photograph,' said Tom. 'There was one like it in my great-uncle's house when I visited Oakley Mill as a young boy. He died a year or two ago.'

'Freddie Crane, Grandad's best friend.'

'He told you about him?'

'He's talked about him, yes. He asked me to collect the photo from his cottage and take it in tomorrow.'

'And that's his cottage over there?'

She looked across the road and nodded. His intent look lasted so long, she wondered what he was thinking. 'He and my grandmother moved there a couple of years ago,' she said sadly. 'They loved it.'

'I don't wonder. It's a beautiful spot.'

She re-wrapped the photograph, feeling stronger now. 'I must go.'

'I'll walk along with you.'

'Thank you.' She was glad of his company and when he left her at the door of *Love-in-a-Mist* she felt bereft in a way she hadn't expected.

* * *

Afterwards, Alice couldn't remember much of the hours that followed the phone call from the hospital. It came early the next morning: her grandfather had died peacefully in his sleep.

'But he can't have,' had been her instant reaction. 'He wanted a special photograph. I was bringing it in for him today.'

After that, everything was hazy; she remembered insisting that Megan carry on with her cookery class as planned, and not cancel it as had been her intention. And she was aware that Harry had been there for her. Alice, dazed, had been so glad of Harry's support and encouragement, carrying her through everything that needed to be done. The funeral director would

169

have driven her to register the death, but this was something she wanted to do on her own. Then there were her grandfather's belongings to collect from the hospital. She took them to the cottage, his last home, to deal with later.

The cremation was booked for a morning in the following week, with a thanksgiving service in church that afternoon. The vicar was kindness itself and for the first time since hearing the news Alice felt tearful. He pressed a tissue into her hand and left her alone for a little while until she felt able to cope.

Both Megan and Harry decided that she should spend the rest of the day with them at Rose Lodge, although she knew she must return to her own apartment after the evening meal because there was Pickles to consider.

'Remember, we're just at the end of the phone,' Megan told her when she pulled up outside *Love-in-a-Mist* after driving her back. 'Shall I come in with you now?'

Alice shook her head.

'I'm fine, really, but thanks. You and Harry are the best friends anyone could have,' she said fervently. 'I don't know what I'd do without you.'

Megan looked solemn. 'Look after yourself, Alice. See you in the morning.'

Alice stood waving until the car was out of sight, and went indoors, climbing the stairs to the flat slowly. Then, remembering that Pickles was still outside, she went down again and let him in.

She picked him up and hugged him close. For once, he lay still in her arms as she carried him up to the flat. As she went in, she felt the rumble of a purr in his soft body, and buried her face in his thick fur for comfort.

9

Alice awoke next morning as daylight was beginning to filter through her bedroom curtains. She lay for a while, thinking of her grandfather and the encouragement he had given her when the idea of taking on *Love-in-a-Mist* had first come to her. If it wasn't for him, she doubted whether she would have continued to think seriously about it, and Megan certainly wouldn't have become involved.

'It's the best thing I've ever done,' Megan had exclaimed after her first group baking session, when the students had gone home full of praise for the amenities *Love-in-a-Mist* offered. 'Or *almost* the best thing,' she had added quickly.

Alice had laughed at her, happy that their plans seemed to be working out even if it was early days.

But now everything felt different. The empty hours stretched ahead of her. There was no longer any hospital visiting, and since Megan's group presented no problems she didn't even have to stay on the premises today in case she was needed. Instead, she could work at her painting anywhere she chose and for as long as she liked, except that there seemed no point to that any more.

She sighed, thinking of the cottage on the seafront and her grandfather's wish that it should eventually provide a home for her that was all her own. Pickles might be pleased to live there again so that he could come in and out of the cat flap as he pleased. She glanced across at her travelling clock on the chest of drawers. It was early yet, but he might be glad to be let out into the freedom of the garden.

He was sitting by the garden door downstairs, but didn't turn his head when he heard her. His back arched a little in what seemed like annoyance.

She unlocked the door and opened it. 'There you are, my lad, the outside world is all yours,' she said.

But he didn't move. She bent to stroke him and a purr started to rumble deep in his soft body. In the end, she went out into the garden with him, standing on the edge of the paving stones that made up the small patio area so that her slippers remained dry. The breezy air smelt of damp grass and of mignonette from the flowerbed in the corner. She took deep breaths of it and the freshness on her face was soothing.

After a while, Pickles wandered back and rubbed himself round her ankles. 'Hungry now?' she said. 'Me too.'

After breakfast she spent some time tidying the flat, and then went down again to unlock the door into the street. People were walking about now, cars grinding up the hill, and there was an air of urgency about the place that hadn't been there half an hour earlier. The working day was getting started. Soon Megan would be here to get things ready for her Friday class, and check she had everything needed for the alfresco lunch recipes she had planned for the session today.

She gazed round at the space that tomorrow would be full of the members of her art group. In the circumstances, people would have understood if she had cancelled, and she wondered now what had made her decide to go ahead, feeling as she did. Some spark of obstinacy, perhaps; a wish not to seem weak. Or maybe the fear that once one group had been cancelled, it would be all too easy to give up entirely?

There was a tap on the door and it opened to reveal Tom, his thick hair ruffled by the breeze.

She looked at him in surprise and saw that he was gazing at her as if he didn't quite know what to say.

'Tom?'

'I had to come. I've only just heard about your grandfather.'

'Yes, well . . . '

'I'm so sorry, Alice.' He hesitated. 'I don't want to intrude, but if there's anything I can do to help . . . I just wanted you to know . . . '

She hoped he wouldn't say that her grandfather had had a good life, that he was very ill and she wouldn't want him to suffer any more, or . . .

'Natalie asked me to extend her condolences to you too.'

She swallowed. 'Thank you for coming. It was good of you, Tom. I'm all right, really. I can cope.' Her words sounded cold and unfeeling, but she couldn't help it. Her grief was private and she could manage.

'You're not alone?'

'Not for long,' she said. 'Here's Megan coming now.'

'Then I'll leave you. But remember what I said, Alice; any time.'

'Any time for what?' Megan demanded as she came in with her arms full of Tupperware boxes.

'Tom offered his help,' said Alice, holding open the kitchen door for her so she could dump her cargo on the table.

'His *help*?'

'That's what he said.'

'And you believed him?'

'Why not?'

Megan frowned. 'It didn't occur to you that he wanted to get in quickly — in case you decide to give up this place, now you'll have somewhere else to live? He wants his name on the top of the waiting list. I hope you put him right about that.'

'You're too suspicious for your own good.'

'But not for yours, Alice, my friend.' Megan looked at her kindly and then gave her a quick hug. 'We need to look out for you, Harry and me, and guard your interests until you're in a fit state to look after yourself.'

'I know,' Alice mumbled as Megan released her. 'What would I do without you? You're great, the pair of you.'

'You shouldn't be doing too much too soon,' said Megan, her voice stern.

'You need to get away for a bit. Too bad I'm involved with my lot this morning, but we'll do something fantastic this afternoon; somewhere right away from here to give you a break for a few hours. I told them yesterday that I needed to finish early, and they're happy to take their lunches off to eat at home. What d'you say?'

Alice smiled and agreed. She was anxious now to be out of the way before people began to come in, talking and laughing and demanding to know exactly what Megan had in mind for them to start doing this morning.

'Think up somewhere good,' said Megan as she took the lid off the largest box. 'You provide the ideas and I'll provide a delicious lunch. Deal?'

'Deal,' said Alice. 'And thanks.'

Upstairs again, she wandered across to the kitchen window and stared out at the garden. Beyond, the sea looked like a sheet of pearly silk. She wished she could forget Megan's censorious words about Tom's likely motive for being here so quickly. Not that she believed it for an instant, of course, but Megan could be very persuasive.

But give up *Love-in-a-Mist*? No way. Her earlier feelings about the unimportance of everything to do with it had quite vanished, and she had Megan to thank for that. Together they made a good team. Harry, too, could hardly be more supportive. What had she been thinking of earlier? It had been her grandfather's hope that she would find fulfilment here, and she'd be letting down his memory if she gave up now.

She picked up the hymn book the vicar had lent her so she could choose her grandfather's favourite hymns for the service. Out in the garden, she sat down on the low wall and opened the book. Grandad had loved the sea, and she knew he liked *Eternal Father, Strong to Save*. How did it go on? *Whose arm hath bound the restless wave* ... Yes, that was it. And how about *Who Would True Valour See*, and *Amazing Grace*? She thumbed through the book, and then returned to her original ideas, content with what she had chosen. She hadn't produced the hymn book when she was at Rose Lodge, preferring to be on her own when she decided.

Later, she would contact the vicar again. She had plenty to attend to for now. There were things that needed doing out there in the garden, weeding and suchlike. And the roses could do with some dead-heading. She could be busy all morning doing something useful, and at the same time thinking of somewhere to go this afternoon that would please Megan.

Her grandparents had loved the Devon fishing village of Beer, not many miles away along the coast, and Grandad's last trip with her had been there. So what better place for a sunny summer afternoon? They could visit the latest exhibition in the Marine Gallery, and the Steam Gallery, too. Maybe she would even find some inspiration there for her own paintings.

* * *

The village of Beer was always full of surprises. Its long, narrow street leading down to the beach, with the stream burbling down alongside, was as bright and interesting as ever. But today there were lines of bunting from one side to the other all the way down, and an air of expectancy about the place that was uplifting.

'So what's going on?' said Megan.

Crowds had begun to gather at the bottom where the road ran steeply down to the sea. Several fishing boats were pulled up on the beach and the cliffs on either side were bright in the sunshine.

'A regatta?' Alice said.

'Canoe racing,' someone said close by. 'You'll see them in a minute.'

'A lot of fuss for a few canoes,' Megan muttered in Alice's ear. 'We've got canoes at home. Bigger and better ones too.'

Alice smiled. 'Let's go up on the top

there and see what's what.' She pointed up to the left where her grandfather had liked to sit and look at the view.

Megan groaned. 'It's steep.'

'It's not too bad. I can see an ice-cream van.'

'In that case, you're on.'

They sat eating huge cornets crammed with strawberry ice-cream. Megan gave a sigh of pleasure as she finished hers and wiped her mouth with the tissue provided. She looked round for a bin.

'Over there,' said Alice, tossing hers towards it.

Megan's didn't quite reach; grumbling, she got up to deal with it.

'You need more practice,' Alice said, smiling.

'Phew!' Megan sitting down again and leaning back in her seat. 'You didn't warn me it was going to be so hot.' She pulled out a tissue to wipe her damp forehead. This time her aim for the bin was successful.

Alice was beginning to regret not

wearing a light summery skirt instead of her jeans. 'We could move out of the sun,' she said.

A cry went up from down below as a host of canoeists came round the end of the headland all wearing orange life jackets and moving swiftly towards the beach. At the same moment a crowd of people appeared suddenly in front of Alice and Megan to lean on the railings for a better view.

Megan jumped up. 'Come on, then, the galleries it is.'

It was cool inside, and they spent a happy time admiring the exhibits in both places. Then, they went in search of coffee and found a small café in a side street.

'*Pool of Dreams*,' Megan said, gazing up at the sign hanging above their heads. 'This looks all right.' She also liked the window display of waterfowl around a pond, looking so lifelike she had to dip her finger in to check it wasn't real water.

Alice sat back in her corner seat and

watched her, smiling. Several small moorhens on the bank seemed as if they would like to follow their parent into the water, but didn't quite know how to set about it.

Megan picked one up and looked at it in surprise. 'It feels so light,' she said. 'I thought it would be heavier, as it's made of metal. And look at the exquisite markings on it, and the realistic colour.'

'It's a work of art.'

'I want one of these.'

'It's not for sale,' Alice said, pointing to a notice to that effect.

Megan put the moorhen back on the bank with reluctance. 'I really like it.' She picked up another and turned it over to see the maker's name. 'Oakley Designs,' she read. 'I wonder where I could buy one of these?'

'I'd like to know too,' said the waitress, coming to serve them. She looked neat in her short green-and-white-patterned dress. 'I'm working on it. These were here when we took over a couple of weeks ago.'

'So you're new here, then?' said Megan, interested.

'My brother and I own the place now. Ivan and Olivia Dream. He's off to the garden centre today, to find out what he can about pond maintenance — for the real one in the back garden we've inherited. I thought he'd be back by now.'

'I like your window display,' said Megan.

Olivia looked pleased. 'Nice, isn't it? I'd like to buy more of these little fellows for the garden pond. We're planning a sitting-out area out at the back, you see, with the pond in the centre as the main feature. We'll need to stock it with fish, of course.'

At once, Megan became involved in professional catering talk, and for the moment the order for coffee was forgotten. Alice, resigned, looked round the pretty room and then got up to examine some of the watercolours on the pale green walls. All of them were of water scenes in subtle tones of mauve and pale green, and featured waterfowl. The whole effect was charming, and it was a shame that they were the only customers on a sunny early summer day. But the place had an old-fashioned air about it that perhaps was off-putting.

At last, Olivia remembered why they were here. She pushed a stray lock of fair hair behind her ear and whipped a pad and pencil out of her pocket.

'Toasted teacake for me,' said Megan. 'For you too, Alice? Oh, and chocolate fudge cake, please, and coffee as well.'

'I'll be right back,' said Olivia, poised for flight.

'No hurry,' said Megan.

Olivia smiled. 'Maybe when you've finished you might like a look at what we're doing outside?'

'You've made a new friend there,' Alice said when she had gone.

Megan grinned. 'What a find this place is. I'm glad we came. You learn something new every day. And I told her what we're doing at *Love-in-a-Mist*. It's given her a few ideas as well.'

Alice was glad to see her friend looking so happy and animated. She was enjoying the outing too, and grateful to Megan for suggesting they came away from Lyme for a few hours this sunny afternoon. Now she must do her bit and get on with her life in the only way she knew — a lot of hard work, determined *Love-in-a-Mist* would be the success they dreamed of.

On the journey home Alice allowed herself only a few moments thought about the charming metal moorhens they had admired. She had known at once whose work they were, of course, and was interested to see what kind of thing Tom produced, but decided not to say anything that might spoil Megan's pleasure in them. She wondered where Tom made his sculptures, and if he was still involved with the production of moorhens and other things too. He would need a workshop for that.

'You're very quiet, Alice, my friend,'

Megan said as they joined the main road and headed for Lyme.

'Just thinking,' said Alice.

'Not brooding?'

'Grateful to you for this afternoon, Megan.'

'Don't you think that *Pool of Dreams* needs a boost of something or other to get it going?' said Megan. 'I've a good mind to come up with a few useful ideas for it myself.'

'Such as?'

Megan wrinkled her nose. 'An open morning like we had . . . free coffee and cakes on the lawn. Competitions for children on water birds, fishing in the pond.'

'For what? There aren't any fish in there yet, unless Olivia's brother arrives back with a tank full of them.'

'That could be arranged. Artificial ones, perhaps.'

'That's crazy.'

'I'll think up something else, then, and get back to Olivia.'

'As long as you don't neglect

Love-in-a-Mist.'

Megan was indignant. 'As if!'

'I'll believe you.'

'I hate to see anyone messing things up because they're going about it in the wrong way,' said Megan. 'They'd have a lot going for them if they thought things through and did their research.'

'But we can't interfere.'

'I'm not so sure. I think Olivia would be open to suggestions. But don't worry. I'm not going to neglect *Love-in-a-Mist.*'

Alice smiled, knowing Megan wouldn't do that. She was the one tempted to let things slide, but that must change immediately. Hard work on her part would help her get through these first difficult days, and then she must think about booking another tutor as soon as possible. Already Suzie had been asking who the next one would be and suggesting they book Torville again to demonstrate in a different medium. He was certainly popular with everyone. Even the disgruntled Monica had lightened up and enjoyed herself.

'I'm thinking of who I'll choose as our next monthly tutor,' she said.

'Not Torville Satterly?' Megan said.

'What's wrong with him?'

'Sweet Alice . . . that's what he called you. I heard him laying it on thick that first morning.'

'And how did he describe you? '*Another* beauty'.'

Megan giggled. 'It's great to be appreciated. Maybe you should have him back.'

'Anyway, we need a different tutor each month. That's the whole idea, and what we said in the advertising.'

'We could change our minds.'

'You mean you'd actually be *disappointed* if I don't invite Torville again?'

'Wouldn't *you* be disappointed, too?' said Megan, sounding smug. 'Anyway, I like living dangerously.'

★　★　★

When her grandparents had moved into the small terraced cottage on the seafront, their first Sunday had been special for them: Alice had come to visit before setting out for her new life in Crete. Alice thought of this with poignancy on Sunday morning as she set up her easel on the lawn, in the spot from where she got the best view of the bay. Today, as then, the church bells were ringing and there was a gentle breeze stirring her hair.

They had gone together to the morning service, she remembered, and afterwards Gran had insisted on walking out along the Cobb to the very end, stumbling a little on the cobbled ground. She had been glad of Alice's arm, and as they walked she had wanted to know every detail of her granddaughter's new job in the tourist office, and of the two rooms above the taverna on the seafront where Alice would be living.

'So different from here,' Gran had murmured, gazing out across the harbour where the receding tide had left several boats high and dry.

Now Alice thought of the sparkling blue sea at Elounda, and the ferry boats lined up on the quay, ready to set out for the island of Spinolonga. She thought of George, too, and his older brother Nikos. They owned one of the boats between them, and they had become her good friends. It seemed after a while that Nikos would become more than that to her — but it was not to be. It was hard to remember now exactly how it had been between the two of them, or even what he looked like, when visions of Tom's tanned face and blue eyes insisted on coming into her mind instead.

Frowning, she picked up her paint-brush, but it was hard to concentrate. The funeral was on Monday, and until that was over it was impossible to do any more painting. Instead, she went up to her flat and sorted through her wardrobe until she found the black jacket she had worn at Gran's funeral.

With it, she had teamed her new black trousers and a plain white blouse. Grandad had liked her in bright colours, but on this occasion black suited her mood; and so black it would be.

★ ★ ★

The room, in a building near the church, was prettily decorated in colours to lift the spirits, and the tables laden with sandwiches, quiches and cakes looked attractive. Alice smiled as, with Megan beside her, she welcomed everyone and helped some of the more infirm elderly to find suitable seats.

The service in the church where her grandparents had worshipped had been uplifting in a way she hadn't expected. She was surprised, too, at the number of people who were here, having obviously seen the announcement in the local paper.

Torville gripped her hand afterwards as she stood at the church door and then patted her kindly on the shoulder. 'Dear Alice,' he said, in a voice hushed for the occasion.

Tom, looking distinguished in a black suit and seeming a little remote on this sad occasion, had looked at her intently as he took her hand. She wanted, suddenly, to be held by him, and for a moment they seemed to be the only ones at the church door. Then others crowded behind, people who had known her grandfather and wanted a word with her.

She had arranged for refreshments to be available in this nearby hall as it specialised in funeral teas. The two waitresses were attentive, pouring tea and coffee, and pleasant chat filled the room. Grandad would have been pleased.

She let the sound flow over her, and was only aware that Tom had arrived when Harry got up to offer him his seat at her table.

'No, please,' Tom remonstrated. 'I'm here for only a moment.'

'Then sit down for only a moment,' Harry said. 'I shall hand round some plates at that table over there. They seem to need some help.'

Megan raised her eyebrows at Alice as Tom sat down beside her. At once, a waitress was there pouring tea.

'So how are you?' Tom asked as she moved on.

'I'm relieved it's nearly over.'

'A fine service, if I may say so.'

She nodded. 'Everyone has been so kind.'

'So what will you do now?'

She looked at him in surprise. 'What should I do? The same as always . . . doing my best for *Love-in-a-Mist*, painting . . . '

'You'll be living there permanently?'

She hesitated, not quite liking the way this conversation was going. She was glad that Megan was occupied with her neighbour on the other side of her and hadn't caught the drift of it. 'Why do you ask?'

He picked up his cup, looked at it

thoughtfully and then put it down again. He was silent for so long that she began to wonder what he was planning to say. Then an elderly man, struggling to his feet at the next table, stumbled a little and would have fallen if Tom hadn't leapt to his assistance.

After that, one or two people started to leave, and Alice got up to say goodbye. Others were moving now too, and as they said their long farewells to people they hadn't seen for years, Alice realised that Tom had slipped away too.

'At least your friend Torville didn't turn up to the tea,' said Megan, when at last the three of them were alone.

'He has his sensitive side.'

Megan flopped down in her seat again and reached for a meringue. 'It all went very well, Alice. Now you can relax.'

But Alice didn't want to relax. She was filled now with determination to work all hours, but she wouldn't tell Megan that Tom's attitude might have had a lot to do with it.

★ ★ ★

'What a day to choose,' Megan wailed the next morning, when she arrived at *Love-in-a-Mist* straight from her shopping expedition to prepare for the cream teas. 'We'll have to set up inside just in case anyone is mad enough to turn up in weather like this, but I wouldn't bet on it.'

Alice surveyed the trays of freshly-baked scones on the table. 'It's a waste of effort if they don't,' she said.

'We'll have to stick them in the freezer and use them up in the coffee breaks at your workshop — if anyone's prepared to eat them,' Megan said. 'Unless, of course, Danny turns up after school to help us out.'

'He might just do that, rain or no rain.'

'It looks as if it'll rain for the rest of the week. And we're doing this every afternoon! How did we come to make that mad decision? The stress of it all will kill us.'

But they were both taken aback by the turnout. By the time Danny appeared after school, the place was heaving.

He came into the kitchen, round-eyed with surprise. 'What's going on here, then?' he said, shedding his jacket.

'It's too wet to use the lawn today,' said Megan. 'Better luck tomorrow.' She looked exhausted as she flopped down on a handy stool.

'The numbers are easing off a bit now, but it's been like it all afternoon,' said Alice. 'You get off home, Megan. Danny and I can manage now, can't we, Danny?' Already he had picked up an empty tray to clear some of the tables. 'I don't know what we'd do without you,' she told him, exhausted.

He grinned as he vanished through the door. 'Just make sure there's one of those huge scones left for me.'

'And jam and cream?'

But he'd gone.

Later, pouring a mug of tea for him at the kitchen table, Alice heard a rattle at the outside door and got up to investigate. She found Tom outside.

He came in, his curly hair darkened by moisture. 'I'm looking for Danny. Have you seen him?'

'You've come to the right place,' she said.

He looked relieved, but was still frowning.

'He's here.' She led the way into the kitchen. She refused to feel in the wrong, although from his demeanour Tom looked as if he thought she had kidnapped his charge against the boy's will.

'Hi, Tom,' said Danny. 'We've been busy here this afternoon.'

'*All* the afternoon?'

'Since school finished. How many covers were there, Alice?'

She smiled. 'You sound like a professional.'

Danny looked pleased. 'I'm coming again tomorrow for more practice.'

'Don't be too sure of that,' said Tom, his voice sharp.

'But I'm needed here,' Danny protested. 'Megan said so. We've done pretty well today, haven't we, Alice?'

'Brilliantly, considering the weather.'

'She's sold some more of her paintings too.'

'So that's why there are spaces in the window?' Tom said.

'I'm working as hard as I can,' Alice said with dignity.

'Not hard enough if you're selling well.'

She stared back at him, stony-faced.

'Not my business, I know,' he said, as if he could read her thoughts. 'But anything Danny is involved in concerns me. I don't want him overworked.'

Alice glanced at the boy, spreading cream on his scone with evident enjoyment. 'Does he look overworked?'

'Well, no. I'll give you that.'

'Well, then?'

'He has his homework to do.'

'Done it,' said Danny with his mouth full.

'All of it?'

'Pretty much.'

Tom looked suspicious. 'When was this?'

Danny shrugged. 'At dinner time, of course. That's when we all do it.'

'So that's why you're starving?' said Alice.

'Me? I'm always starving.'

Alice glanced at Tom, trying not smile. 'I'm not sure we like our staff to arrive here undernourished.'

Suddenly his displeasure vanished. 'Sorry. I deserved that. I was overreacting, and totally out of order given the circumstances.'

'Then he's got a reprieve?'

'I was afraid for his safety, that's all. He's too keen on doing risky things for my peace of mind. I feared the worst.'

'He'll be quite safe here,' Alice promised, smiling.

Tom's eyes crinkled in answer as he smiled too. 'I don't doubt that for a moment, but I don't want him making things harder for you. Don't be late then, Danny, and don't eat them out of house and home. I've got Natalie waiting, so I must be off. I'll get back to work for an hour or two. Meet me there, Danny, and then we'll go for something to eat, as you're apparently starving. OK?'

Danny nodded. 'OK.'

When Tom had gone Danny wiped his mouth with the back of his hand and grinned.

'D'you often do risky things?' asked Alice.

'Sometimes.'

'What sort of things?'

'Climbing, abseiling.'

'Not on these cliffs here?' said Alice, horrified. 'Don't you know they're unsafe?'

He looked at her pityingly. 'In Cornwall, near Land's End where I went with Dad before he went off. It's fossils here, not climbing. I found some good ones at the weekend. Tom was impressed.'

Alice was silent, thinking about Danny's parents and his need now to be living here with Tom. She couldn't ask exactly why, of course, but her sympathy for the boy deepened. He took everything in such a matter-of-fact way, and got on with things as best he could. It was obvious that he and his uncle got on well together — but what about Natalie? Somehow, she couldn't believe that Natalie would take kindly to having a young boy in tow taking up Tom's time and attention.

'Any more cake?' asked Danny hopefully.

Alice laughed. 'What was it Tom said . . . not to eat us out of house and home? Don't tell me you're still starving?'

He grinned. 'A try-on, that's all,' he admitted.

'It's not going to work.'

'It doesn't with Tom, either,' he said.

★   ★   ★

Danny wished that Tom's workplace was anywhere but attached to Natalie

Tanner's tiny cottage near Western Beach. A tumbledown outhouse with a corrugated tin roof that sounded like thunder even in the lightest shower of rain wasn't exactly his idea of a perfect place for running a business. It smelt of old sacks and animal food — although no animal had been near the place for years, Natalie told him. Danny wasn't surprised. No self-respecting animal would want to doss down on *her* premises.

But, surprisingly, the workshop was well-equipped with power points, and that suited Tom for the time being. So did the massive workbench along the longest wall, and the good access for deliveries. He had important orders to meet, big ones, and this was the best place he could come up with until they were all dispatched. Then he'd have time to look around and get onto the Internet for some research.

'I'd do this for you, easy,' Danny had said a week ago but Tom had said it was his problem and he would deal with it in his own way and in his own good time, thank you very much.

That was all very well, but the trouble was that Natalie made it plain she didn't want him to leave.

Danny caught sight of Natalie, now busy at the kitchen sink; but, thanks to a bit of luck, she hadn't seen him. He could hear the machinery at work in the workshop as he approached, and knew that Tom would be too engrossed to want him interrupting for the moment. He was early, anyway.

Dragging his feet, he slouched round to the front of the cottage, intending to slip inside without Natalie seeing him so he could turn on the TV in the sitting-room and watch *Eggheads*. After that he would investigate the channels to see if anything interesting came up. It would pass a bit of time, anyway.

He settled himself in a big armchair, leaned back and closed his eyes.

'What are you doing in here?' Tom's voice sounded loud in the quiet room as Danny woke with a start.

He rubbed his eyes. 'Waiting for you,' he mumbled.

'In Natalie's private sitting-room?'

Danny saw that she had followed Tom in and had slotted her arm through his.

'And why shouldn't he?' she said. 'It's only right that Danny should feel at home, Tom, as much as you do.'

Tom nodded but he didn't smile. 'Get yourself out of here then, Danny,' he said. 'And we'll be on our way.'

'No need,' said Natalie, releasing her arm and smiling up at Tom. 'There's a casserole in the oven, your favourite chicken recipe, Tom. Enough for all three of us, of course. We're like a real family now.'

Danny could see that Tom was in a quandary. If he'd been him he'd have come straight out and refused, but Tom was too polite for that. The moment was awkward and it felt like his fault.

'I've got my project to finish,' he said. 'It's back at the mill. I've got to have it done by tomorrow.'

Tom flashed Natalie a bright smile. 'Lead the way then, Danny, and no messing about. Sorry, Natalie. Another time perhaps.'

His hand on Danny's shoulder was heavy, but Danny didn't complain. He was filled with triumph that he'd won a victory even though he'd had to lie to do it. He wasn't sure if Tom realised that, but he wasn't going to let on. The only difficulty was producing evidence of this project that was so vital to have completed; but he'd think of something on the drive back to the chalet behind Oakley Mill.

10

The last person Alice expected to see an evening or two later, as she walked along the path by the river with her sketching things in her shoulder bag, was Torville Satterly: seated on a bench with his head bowed over a large pad of paper.

For a moment she hardly recognised him in his broad-brimmed hat and trimmer clothes than last time, but then he jerked his head round at her approach.

His face lit up into a beaming smile. 'Alice, my dear Alice!'

'Torville.'

He patted the seat beside him. 'Sit down and take the weight off your feet. Not that there's much of that, by the look of you.'

'I'm searching for a good place to sketch,' she said, not moving. 'Further up by the bridge, I thought.'

'It's better here,' he said. 'Look at those eddies on the water, and the way the branches hang over with those interesting reflections.'

She glanced at where he indicated, and saw patterns and shapes that were continually changing. He had obviously seen them and appreciated them too, because the charcoal sketches on his pad looked impressive.

'Something bad's happened, hasn't it?' he said. 'Sit down and tell your Uncle Torville all about it.'

There was such kindness in his voice that Alice's throat felt tight as she sat down and put her bag down at her feet. For a moment she couldn't speak. And then it came pouring out: all about her grandmother's illness that had brought her hastening back from Elounda only just in time to see her before she died, and then her decision to remain here to be near her grandfather because he needed her.

'I spent a lot of time with them when

I was little after my father died,' she said, 'And they were everything to me some years later when my mother remarried and moved to South America.'

'And your grandfather now?'

'He died,' she said. 'He was ill for some time.'

'My poor, poor girl.'

She gazed at the flowing water in front of them through misty eyes. The grassy bank on the other side looked blurred, and she watched as something she couldn't immediately recognise moved amidst the foliage. Then she saw it was a pigeon. A moment later, it flew off with a great flapping of wings.

She pulled out a tissue to wipe her eyes. Torville's presence next to her was a surprising comfort after his previous brash behaviour. He sat motionless, his large hands in his lap and the brim of his hat hiding part of his face, so she was unable to read his expression. It had been easy to misjudge him when he came blustering into *Love-in-a-Mist* to tutor the group the other day. Now she was seeing him as he really was. Or was this an act, too?

She screwed her tissue into a tight ball and stuffed it in her pocket. Immediately he produced another.

'Thanks,' she said, taking it. 'I'm all right now.'

'No-one's all right,' he said soberly. 'Not all the time. Not most of the time, in so many cases.'

'That sounds depressing.'

'Bad attitude is depressing, good attitude is inspiring. That lady in the wheelchair . . . '

'Suzie?'

'Now, she's a one. I like *her*.'

'You didn't seem to notice her much at the workshop.'

'Why should I? She was one of the group getting on with things. She wouldn't have thanked me for singling her out, now, would she?'

Alice laughed shakily. 'You're right.'

'I'm always right.'

'And modest with it too?'

A deep, rumbling laugh shook

Torville's stout frame. He caught hold of her hand and pressed it. 'Always at your service, dear Alice.'

'It's good to have friends,' she said. 'I don't know what I'd do without Megan's friendship, and her husband's too. They're great.'

'She has a shadow in her eyes sometimes, poor girl,' Torville said.

'Not often,' said Alice. It humbled her to realise that he had picked up on that hint of sadness in Megan when most people didn't.

He sighed. 'I got off on the wrong foot with her, I'm afraid. I do that sometimes. And, talking of feet, I've finished here. Let's wander along up river to that bridge of yours and do some work up there.'

She agreed at once. As they walked, they talked of perspective in drawing, but Alice had the feeling he was referring to something deeper that would give her a lot to think about afterwards. Meanwhile, she concentrated on what she had come out for this evening.

Torville waited until she had chosen the view she liked best. 'That's an interesting spot,' he said. 'A little obvious, perhaps, but we'll see what you make of it.' He gave her a pat on the arm for encouragement, then crossed the bridge to a bank of trees on the other side and disappeared among them.

One or two people passed, but Alice found she could work easily enough knowing that Torville was there somewhere, although she couldn't see him. The water, wider here, flowed serenely, and the evening light gave subtle tones to the overhanging branches. She resolved to return here again at different times of the day so that she could catch the light in other ways too.

After a while, a slight rustling alerted her to Torville's return. She smiled to see him come lumbering back towards her across the bridge.

'Can I see what you've been doing?' she asked.

'That's what I should be asking you,'

he said. 'You first.'

Such was his kind interest that she didn't mind showing him; although she wasn't quite sure she had captured the scene as she wanted it, because something about it didn't look quite right.

He said nothing for the moment. Then he smiled. 'Well done. Just a little change here and there, d'you mind?'

She handed him her charcoal. 'Go ahead.'

Fascinated, she saw him make just a few adjustments that made all the difference. She looked at him in awe. 'You're a good teacher.'

'You've noticed?'

'There you go again in your modesty.'

He laughed and she laughed with him. 'Now show me yours, Torville,' she said.

He had chosen an unusual view of the bridge that was hardly noticeable among the trees and bushes. Instead, he had concentrated on a crooked root obtruding from the bank and its reflections in the water. The effect was stunning.

'Brilliant,' she said.

He closed his sketch pad. 'You get an eye for it. You learn to look. Practise, practise, practise.'

'It's what we try to do at our workshops. Will you come and tutor us again, and perhaps bring us all up here to sketch outdoors, weather permitting? I'm sure we'll get a few takers.'

He looked pleased. 'Why not, dear Alice?'

And so it was arranged, and another day of the week chosen for this special event so that it didn't clash with their studio work.

'And I have something to ask of you now, if you'll be so kind to a struggling artist,' he said, smiling broadly. 'Will you come to the preview of my exhibition in Lyme next Saturday? The Cobb Hall, six till eight?'

Alice smiled. 'I'd love to. An exhibition of your own paintings?'

'One or two.' His eyes twinkled at her. 'Modest enough for you?'

'I'll want to see more than one or two.'

'You will,' he promised.

'Then I'll be there.'

★　★　★

Alice found herself thinking a lot about the Satterly exhibition in the days that followed, and she made a point of mentioning the event at both the painting workshops that week. Most of those present had seen the flamboyant posters dotted about the town and promised to be there.

'There's good wheelchair access,' said Suzie's friend, Brian, at the Wednesday group. His voice rang with enthusiasm.

'You'd have to carry me in otherwise,' said Suzie, laughing up at him. 'I've simply got to be there too.'

By Saturday evening, Alice had worked on her oil painting of the bridge, and was fairly pleased with it. She looked forward to showing the finished work to Torville on Monday before they set out for the sketching trip along the riverbank with the rest of the group. But meanwhile, there was the preview of his exhibition to think about.

She dressed carefully, more light-hearted than she had been for days. Checking in the full-length mirror in her bedroom, she saw that her blue-flowered dress suited her, and its length was just right with the high, strappy sandals.

She set out early feeling a sense of anticipation as she walked carefully up the hill to The Cobb Hall. Torville, resplendent in tuxedo and red cummerbund, welcomed her at the door with a friendly hug.

'Alice!' he said, holding her at arm's length to take a good look at her. 'Even more beautiful than ever.'

Her face felt warm with colour as she tried to step to one side, others coming in behind her, but Torville was having none of it. 'Not so fast,' he said. 'I need you at my side, dear Alice.'

There was nothing for it but to acquiesce. She was aware of someone standing behind her, and turned to see Tom, frowning heavily, with Danny at his side.

'Natalie couldn't come,' Danny whispered to her. He was looking smart in new jeans and navy sweatshirt, and his unruly hair was sleeked down.

'Welcome, young man,' Torville boomed.

'Is this your exhibition?' Danny asked, looking interested. 'I haven't been to one like this before.'

'A personal introduction, then,' said Torville. 'I'll leave my lovely assistant to do the honours and take you round myself.'

'*Assistant?*' said Tom when they had gone. 'Since when have you teamed up with that buffoon?'

Alice looked at him coldly. 'I'm surprised you showed up here, feeling about the artist as you do.'

'I like to keep an eye on the opposition.'

'I don't think there's much opposition between Torville's paintings and your ducks.'

'You've seen them, then?'

A crowd of people arrived at the moment, and Alice smiled as she welcomed them and dealt with a question or two about leaving their coats in the designated place. By the time this was done, Tom had vanished, presumably to join Danny and check that he wasn't being brainwashed by someone he despised.

The place was filling up nicely now, and at last Alice felt she could relinquish her post and join the throng inside. Someone thrust a glass of wine into her hand and pointed out the dishes of nibbles.

Alice picked up an olive and bit into it.

'You won't get fat on that,' said Torville, joining her. 'Have another drink.'

She smiled. 'I need my wits about me to appreciate your work.' she said, looking about her. 'But where is it?'

'Follow me.'

He threaded his way through the throngs of people, a difficult task as most of them wanted to slap him on the back and exchange insults. It wasn't quite what Alice had expected from the evening, but it created an atmosphere of bonhomie that was strangely appealing. They reached the open doorway at last, and she saw that the walls of the next room were ablaze with colour from the huge canvasses on the walls.

'Breathtaking,' she said.

'You like it?' He beamed at her, twisting his bow tie so that it was slightly askew.

She resisted the temptation to straighten it, and looked instead at the nearest painting: a swirl of river eddies in strident greens and blues.

'I love that one.'

'Recognise the spot?'

'Is that where we went the other

evening?' she said in wonder. She hadn't seen it in such glorious Technicolor at the time, but it definitely worked: immediately, she felt herself back there, and could almost hear the flapping of the pigeon's wings.

'I was sorry to discover that your grasp of ornithology is a bit dodgy,' said Tom's voice behind her.

She spun round. 'What d'you mean?'

'The study of birds.'

'I know what ornithology is.'

'Well, then?'

She glared at him.

'What have birds to do with my painting?' Torville demanded. 'I never paint birds. I hate birds. Nasty twittering things.'

Alice laughed.

Another back-slapping group arrived and Torville's attention was diverted. They bore him off with them in a cheerful crowd.

'Twittering ducks,' said Tom reflectively. 'A new one on me.'

'Or twittering moorhens,' said Alice.

'Aha, you knew!'

'I saw some in Beer.'

'Real ones?'

She shook her head. 'I was impressed.'

'Good girl.'

'The owner of *Pond of Dreams* was wondering where she could get some more. Did you know that?'

He smiled. 'She knows Natalie, you know, from their schooldays. Natalie introduced me to her on Wednesday, and Olivia placed an order there and then. That's a nice little place she and her brother have got there, don't you think? It could do with a bit more about it, though.'

'That's what Megan thinks.'

'Ah yes, Megan.' His expression seemed to change as if he would like to have said more, but understood it would not be to her liking. Alice frowned. What was it about her friend that these two men objected to? She couldn't understand it. Megan was lovely, funny and kind, and the best friend anyone could have.

'So you're still in production?' she said.

'With difficulty.'

'I see.'

But of course she didn't see, because she didn't know where he operated from. She looked at him thoughtfully, wanting to ask but not liking to seem too curious. In any case, Torville was back now, taking her arm and propelling her towards yet another room, saying that they should be first at the table where the finger buffet was being served because he liked stuffed mushrooms and there weren't so many of those.

As they reached the doorway, she glanced back at Tom, and saw that he was standing with his back to them: apparently staring at the painting she had admired. The thought occurred to her that he felt lonely among this horde of people he didn't know, and who seemed so taken up with themselves. She wondered where Natalie was this evening that she couldn't be here with him.

He was gone by the time they had finished eating. Leaving Torville still surrounded by a cheerful group, Alice returned to the exhibition room to continue her inspection by herself. There was no doubt that Torville had tremendous talent. He had pointed out some members of the press here tonight, and she hoped they would write good reviews. Torville deserved to be recognised and made much of.

Smiling, she toured the room. She felt exhausted with emotion by the time she had seen and admired all the works. She wished she could paint like this, with such lively and illuminating results. But then every artist was different, she thought, portraying what they saw in their own unique way.

There was a slight commotion in the doorway, and to Alice's delight she saw Suzie in her wheelchair with Brian beside her.

'Alice, my dear!' Suzie cried. 'I'm so

pleased to see you.'

'Me too,' said Brian.

He was almost unrecognisable in his dark suit and white shirt, when she had grown accustomed to his old painting gear. Suzie, too, looked stunning in her long, shimmering dress and crimson wrap.

'How smart you both look,' Alice said.

'You don't look so bad yourself,' said Brian, his eyes gleaming.

'A mutual admiration society,' said Suzie. 'And why not? Look, here are some more of our good friends.'

The new arrivals were members of the workshop group too, but they greeted each other as if they hadn't met for weeks.

The evening was taking on a more relaxed feel now, and Alice found she was enjoying herself. It felt good being among her new friends, and she would have a lot to tell Megan tomorrow when she joined her and Harry at their home for Sunday lunch.

* * *

'Guess what,' said Megan the next day as she transferred a pan of early runner beans to a vegetable dish on the worktop beside her cooker.

They had opted to eat in the garden as the weather was too good to be inside.

'We should have been picnicking on the beach,' said Harry.

'Runner bean sandwiches?' said Megan. 'I don't think so.'

'It'll be lovely out there in the shade,' Alice said. And more peaceful, too, she thought as she gathered the knives and forks and carried them out to the seating area beneath a weeping willow tree.

'Harry called in at Beer on his way home from Exeter yesterday,' Megan said. 'He found *Pool of Dreams*. They've got red cloths on all the tables now, and bright flowers. It looked good, I thought, and I wasn't the only person in there having coffee.'

'Good for Olivia,' said Alice.

It was beautiful here, with the sound of trickling water from the stream in the background. Megan had cooked a chicken dish of her own invention she wanted to try out before using it as one of the recipes for a future cookery class.

'It's wonderful,' said Alice as she took her first delicious mouthful. 'You're a genius, Megan.'

There was peach crumble, to follow made from fresh fruit with a topping of amoretti biscuits and almonds.

'A simple recipe,' said Megan, leaning back in her chair and wiping beads of moisture from her forehead.

Alice glanced anxiously at her as she passed her dish for a second helping and then helped herself to cream. Her friend tired easily these days, and she was afraid she was taking on too much. Her latest idea was a mini-holiday for the keenest members of her cookery groups, touring the West Country in search of local recipes.

'Ridiculous,' Harry had said at once.

'What's wrong with the local recipes we have round here?'

'Over the top,' Alice agreed.

Megan looked disgruntled. 'I thought you were my friend, Alice Milner.'

Alice had smiled. 'That's why.'

So now, when Megan's face lit up with a smile and she sat up straight in a determined sort of way, Alice was apprehensive.

'I'd like to invite Olivia over to *Love-in-a-Mist* one evening and show her round,' Megan said. 'What do you say to that, Alice? She's the owner of that place in Beer, Harry. A simple meal afterwards, already prepared, and then a wander round town. Get some ideas into her head.'

'All right by me,' said Alice.

'I'll give her a ring now,' said Megan, jumping up.

Harry looked resigned. 'OK then, do that while I make coffee. You stay there, Alice. I won't be long.'

Alice adjusted her chair so that she could lean back and gaze up into the branches through the gently rustling leaves. She closed her eyes, thinking of Tom and his temporary studio at Natalie Tanner's place, and her plans to extend it. She was almost asleep when she heard the sound of rattling china, and Megan's voice exhorting Harry to be careful.

She had brought a pad and biro out with her, and when the coffee had been poured she made a list of the things Olivia should know about running a business of which she was probably still unaware.

'She's a lucky girl, having you two on her case,' Harry observed with a cup halfway to his lips. 'But who knows what she might be able to tell you in return?'

Alice smiled as Megan flicked a paper napkin at her husband. 'What could she possibly tell us that we don't already know?' she demanded.

'You might be surprised,' said Harry.

11

'I've brought this for you both,' said Olivia breathlessly, handing Megan something wrapped in white tissue paper. 'A thank you for being so kind.'

'But we've done nothing,' Megan objected.

'Oh, but you have.'

Megan gave cry of delight as she pulled the paper aside and revealed a small metal sculpture of a moorhen.

'You couldn't have given her anything better,' Alice exclaimed.

'It's for you, too, Alice.'

Alice thanked her, but inside she felt dismayed. It was beautiful, of course, but somehow it seemed entirely wrong for *Love-in-a-Mist* — as if it was the first in a long line of metal objects planning on invading their space. She smiled at her fanciful thoughts, but she didn't want it here, reminding her.

'I'll be able to see it when I visit Megan,' she said. 'It'll look good by her garden pond, and who am I to deny the poor little thing some water?'

Olivia giggled. 'I can see you think it's real, just like me. Perfect, isn't it? I was so pleased to be introduced to the manufacturer, even if . . . ' Her face clouded and then cleared again. 'But no matter, I've got my moorhens and that's good.'

Megan, stroking her own and crooning over it, wasn't aware for the moment of what was going on round her, but Alice drew Olivia a little to one side.

'So you've met Tom Carey?' she said.

'Strange, really. They were wandering round Beer, and when he saw my moorhens in the window display he came in. Natalie recognised me at once from our schooldays. I didn't like her then. She was unpopular with all the girls. Somehow, I'm now her new best friend — especially when she found I could place an order for more moorhens, and a couple of storks too, and Tom was happy. She was all over me, prattling on about getting his workshop enlarged at her place.'

Megan, looking up, was incredulous. 'You're Natalie Tanner's best friend?'

'Her best enemy,' said Olivia firmly.

'I'm glad to hear that.'

'You dislike her too?'

'And how,' said Megan with feeling. 'I had more than enough of her at college, I can tell you.'

'And was she a riot among other people's boyfriends there as well?'

'She didn't succeed with Megan's,' Alice said proudly.

Olivia sighed. 'Mine was so lovely. Very quiet, but kind and polite. He didn't know what had hit him. She only did it for a laugh, but it was never the same after that. She was always on the look-out for victims, girls she suspected fancied someone, and in she honed and took over and spoilt everything.'

She looked so sad that Alice hastened to divert her. They had already shown her the large downstairs kitchen where Megan held her classes, and where the scones for the cream teas were made.

'We've tried to be different here, you see,' said Alice. 'We were lucky enough to find a gap in the market. Oil painting classes are thin on the ground, and it seemed a shame when that's what I'm interested in. So I started to think of painting workshops, and then we got more ideas and ran with them. Your place is not the same as here, of course. You've got that fantastic garden.'

Olivia's pale face lit up. 'My brother's pride and joy.'

'There you are, then. Think about it for the moment. How could you make that work for you? How could you get hordes of people through your tea shop and out there eating in the sunshine, but make it different?'

'The pond,' said Olivia dreamily. 'Fish. Wildlife. Ivan to show them round the place answering questions, and me serving meals. He got his degree in horticulture and it's about time he did something with it.'

Megan leaned forward eagerly. 'He could give talks, couldn't he?'

'That's an idea.'

'You'll need to advertise them well in advance. What a pity you can't get to the Satterly exhibition here. All those bright swirling colours on your walls would attract interest — draw people into, and then through, the place.'

'Hey, slow down Megan,' Alice warned. 'We're talking to Olivia here.'

But their new friend seemed fired with enthusiasm. 'I could get Tom Carey back again and see if I can come to some arrangement to sell his things — with some commission for us, of course.'

Megan frowned. 'Tom Carey?'

'And Ivan can come over to Lyme and visit the exhibition tomorrow. You've got me going now.'

'Think it about it carefully before you do anything, won't you, Olivia?' said Alice. She wished they hadn't gone so fast. Megan could be a bit overpowering at times, though with the best of intentions.

Megan was looking pensive now. 'There'll be someone stewarding the exhibition tomorrow because the artist is tutoring one of Alice's groups,' she said.

'We're working outside along the riverbank,' said Alice.

'So Ivan could come and find him there?'

'Why not?'

But Megan didn't seem so keen to impart any more information now, and when Olivia made a move to go, she raised no objections but began to gather up their coffee things and pile them on a tray.

Alice knew what was coming as soon as they had seen Olivia off.

'Tom Carey?' said Megan. 'You must have known.' She turned her back on Alice, carried the tray into the kitchen and banged it down on the table.

'You loved the moorhens when we

saw them in Beer,' said Alice, following her in. 'I didn't want to spoil your pleasure in them.'

Megan carried the cups to the sink. 'You deceived me.'

'Of course I didn't. I didn't tell you who made them, that's all.'

'You'll say it was for my own good,' said Megan bitterly as she turned the taps on full blast.

'So why does it matter who the artist is? It's a beautiful object, a work of art. Can't it speak for itself? You recommended Torville Satterly's work to Olivia, and yet you can't stand the man.'

'Who says I can't?'

Alice was silent, knowing it was no use arguing with her friend in this mood. They didn't often fall out, but when they did it was truly upsetting. She picked up a tea towel and unfolded it.

'Let them drain,' said Megan. 'I'm going home now.'

Alice said nothing more, but when

Megan had gone storming off she took the discarded moorhen out into the dusky garden and placed it on the edge of the patio in a broken piece of the low wall near where Pickles liked to sit sometimes.

'Poor unwanted thing,' she said sadly as she found a place on the wall to sit down.

Pickles came across the grass to join her, sniffed at the new possession; and then, deciding it was no threat, rubbed himself against Alice's bare legs. She had much to think about, and sat there until the darkness stole across the garden and only the shimmer of the sea shone silver in the distance.

★　★　★

All next morning, as she sketched with the group along the riverbank, Alice was on the lookout for a stranger: Olivia's brother. Torville was in his element going back and forth between them all, jollying everyone along. He was wearing a jaunty black-brimmed hat today, and a painting smock that billowed out around him as he walked.

No one could mistake him for anything but an artist; and an eccentric one at that, Alice thought. Maybe Ivan, probably as sensitive and quiet as his sister, had turned up when she wasn't looking, taken one look and been frightened off by Torville's exuberance.

Brian and Suzie had chosen to sketch at the same place Torville had chosen the other evening, where the patch of grass was suitable for the wheelchair. Alice joined them, settling herself down on the folding stool she had brought with her.

'This is fun,' said Suzie.

'Difficult, though,' said Brian, looking at his effort critically.

Alice was finding it difficult too. She tore off a sheet of her sketching pad and thrust it into her bag. 'I don't want Torville to see the mess I've made of that,' she said.

Suzie laughed.

Alice tried again, but her heart wasn't in it. She put her stick of charcoal back into its container and stared at the bubbling river in front of her.

'Something worrying you?' said Suzie.

'I was expecting someone to turn up, and he hasn't,' Alice said.

'Someone special?'

'Not really. The brother of a new friend of ours. They've taken over a café in Beer. Megan wanted him to talk to Torville.'

Alice knew that what she was saying didn't make much sense, but Suzie didn't seem to mind. She worked in silence for a few minutes.

At last, Brian sighed and stood up. 'Mind if I wander off for a few minutes?' he said.

'Not a bit,' said Suzie cheerfully. 'Just come back with a masterpiece.'

When he had gone, she looked at her sketch, her head a little on one side. 'I'm quite pleased with this, you know,' she said. She held it out for Alice to see.

'That's really good,' said Alice.

'For a first effort, perhaps.'

'You've got talent, Suzie.'

'You have, my dear, for so many things. Your wonderful paintings, your go-ahead ideas and the ability to carry them out, for friendship . . . '

'Not friendship,' said Alice.

Suzie looked at her so anxiously that Alice found herself on the verge of tears. She said something of how the disagreement between herself and Megan was upsetting, even though she knew that Megan wouldn't let something like this rankle for long.

'Just give it a little time,' Suzie said.

Alice knew she was right. She smiled. 'It's good to talk.'

'We're here for you, you know,' said Suzie, smiling too. 'Brian is a little concerned you are working too hard, my dear.'

'Not this morning,' said Alice, looking at the page in her sketchbook that was almost blank.

Everyone else seemed so engrossed

that the time passed swiftly, and it was well after the scheduled time when Alice glanced at her watch.

She sprang up. 'Torville will be wanting to get back to his exhibition,' she said.

'I don't think so,' said Suzie calmly. 'Just look at him enjoying himself. But Brian and I have plans for this afternoon and we mustn't linger. It's been an enjoyable experience, my dear, and I know we're not the only ones to think so.'

Alice smiled as she saw most of the others begin to pack up too, and Torville's obvious disappointment that he couldn't prolong the session.

'I'll walk along with you, dear Alice,' he said when everyone was ready to go.

She would rather have walked back on her own, but never mind. The day was clouding up now and she wouldn't be sorry to be indoors.

'So how's the exhibition going, Torville?' she said.

He beamed at her. 'Did you enjoy the other evening?'

'More to the point, did you?'

'You're a sharp one, Alice. It was financially a great success, and so has it been this morning too.'

'But you weren't there.'

'I don't need to be when I have minions ready to step in and help me out. Three canvasses sold and a provisional commission for more. Not bad, eh?'

'Brilliant,' she said. 'But how do you know?'

He pulled a mobile phone out of a pocket in his commodious smock. 'Modern technology,' he said. 'They keep me informed.'

'Of course.'

'And you're my inspiration, dear Alice.'

They had reached the end of the river walk now and stopped dead before taking the short cut up to *Love-in-a-Mist*. 'What do you mean?' she said.

'You inspire me to great things. My

beautiful muse . . . '

This sounded alarming. Saying nothing more, she hurried ahead of him up the hill so fast that she arrived breathless outside *Love-in-a-Mist*, in time to see Megan bidding the last of her baking class farewell.

'Alice!' Torville boomed out. 'You're running away from me.'

She swung round and at once his arms went round her.

She struggled free. 'What are you doing?'

'Leave her alone!' Megan shrieked. She landed Torville a slap on his face that made him reel back in astonishment.

'What's that for?'

Torville's hat was half over his face and gave him the look of a demented scarecrow. It would have been funny if Alice didn't feel weak from what had occurred. She swallowed hard.

Megan laughed, her fury dissipating in seconds.

Torville, affronted, straightened his

hat and took a step back. 'My abject apologies, Alice. I was totally out of order.'

'You were,' Megan agreed, her lips twitching.

Seeing it, Alice laughed too, and immediately felt better. It was just his way. Torville Satterly was a law unto himself.

'Am I forgiven?'

He looked so abject that Alice nodded. 'Of course.'

'But don't do it again,' Megan warned.

'Just as well I was there to protect you,' she muttered as Torville turned away. 'Come inside, for goodness' sake. You look as if you've seen a ghost.'

She propelled Alice ahead of her in to the kitchen and towards one of the stools near the table.

'Have you had lunch?' she asked.

Alice shook her head. 'We went on a bit long. You?'

'We ate in the garden on paper plates. A summer picnic was the theme today, so that was nice and easy. Leftover paninis coming up for you now, and some crab and fennel quiche. Will that do you? I'll get the kettle on.'

Alice hadn't thought she was hungry, but found the food that Megan produced so delicious that she changed her mind. 'You're very kind,' she said.

'No more than you deserve,' said Megan, her voice husky.

It was a relief to be back on good terms again, and Alice drank the coffee that Megan produced, feeling comforted and at peace with herself in a way that she hadn't for weeks. Her eyelids began to droop, and she wanted more than anything to lay her head down on the table and sleep

The clatter of dishes as Megan started to clear away brought her back to consciousness. 'Sorry,' she said. 'I feel so tired all of a sudden.'

'I've got that money to take to the bank,' Megan said as she ran water into the bowl and added washing-up liquid. 'Then Harry wants me to collect some bags of compost from the garden centre. Fancy coming out to our place after that?'

'I was going to paint,' Alice said.

'Give it a rest, why don't you? You look all-in.'

'I think I'll stay here and sleep,' said Alice.

'OK,' said Megan. 'I can see when I'm not wanted.'

But she was smiling, and Alice knew she didn't mean it. The old relationship between them was back.

Alice tried to smile too, but even that was an effort.

'You'd better get off upstairs before you pass out,' said Megan.

* * *

Alice woke as her kitchen clock struck seven o'clock, and sat up in alarm. She had slept for hours but she didn't feel rested. Her head ached and her mouth felt dry. She swung her legs out of bed and stood up. All that time asleep, and she felt no better for it. Megan had gone off hours ago, and she had intended to start a new painting based on the sketching she had done this morning. Or not done, as it turned out.

Sighing, she went into the kitchen to make coffee, then carried it into the sitting-room and stood at the window to drink it while looking down into the back garden. It was quiet . . . too quiet? Since she was at the back of the building that should have been no surprise, but she felt disorientated. Even Pickles purring round her ankles would have been especially welcome at this moment. So where was he when she needed him?

She put her empty mug down on the window, found her jacket and went downstairs.

The wind had picked up now, and the waves breaking on the empty beach down below were bigger than she had seen them for days. She leaned on the railings, watching them surge in and break in flying foam, then run up the sand and dissolve ready for the ones following on behind.

Few people were about: just a couple dog-walking and a jogger, looking red in the face and puffing out a greeting as he passed her.

She looked across at the Cobb, the high wall that bounded the harbour on one side protecting the boats from the onslaught of the waves. They were bobbing about at their moorings, looking as if they were becoming anxious.

She walked on. There was faint drizzle in the blustery air now that felt refreshing on her face as she reached the cobbled part and went further out towards the end of the Cobb. At any other time she would have climbed the steps to the top and walked along there, but not today.

Near the end, she found the rock that jutted out from the wall where her grandparents used to sit and look into the distance, just as she was doing now. But in the gathering gloom the cliffs were hazy and no gulls called.

She got to her feet.

'Alice!'

Startled, she turned so quickly her foot slipped, and she would have fallen if Tom hadn't caught her and steadied her. For a moment she was glad to lean safely against him. His thick jersey felt comforting.

'I saw you back there. I followed you,' he murmured.

'But why?'

'You need looking after. You're not well.'

She pulled herself away. 'I'm fine.'

He nodded. 'I know you are really. But just now . . . '

'I came out for some fresh air.'

'There's plenty of that here.'

She shivered.

'Come on, let's sit down for a bit.'

His voice sounded reassuring, as if it was the most reasonable thing in the world to sit here in this cold wind looking out onto the grey, heaving sea. But she was glad to do as he suggested.

They sat in silence for a while, and then she began to wonder why Tom was here, wandering about Lyme in the gathering dusk without Danny at his side.

'Danny's OK, isn't he?' she asked.

'As right as rain,' he said. 'Enjoying himself at the school barbecue he insisted on helping at. Fancies himself as a chef, that boy. I dropped him off early, and then was at a loose end. Natalie's got something else on to do with work. So here I am.'

'Lucky for me,' said Alice.

'You think so?'

'I might have slipped over the edge into all that deep water if you hadn't caught me.'

'You can't swim?'

'I wouldn't fancy it.'

'Nor me. A pair of cowards, aren't we, not wanting to dive into that icy water?'

She smiled. 'It's not quite what I'm used to.'

'In Crete?'

'Warm blue sea, so clear you can see the tiniest fish darting about.'

'You miss it?'

She considered. 'Sometimes, but it seems like a dream. *Love-in-a-Mist* is my real life now.'

She was surprised that he had learnt that much about her. She didn't even know for sure where he lived, even though Danny had hinted once or twice that Oakley Mill featured somewhere in that.

'So you're just waiting around to collect Danny,' she said.

'That's about it. I saw you from right back there, walking very slowly. There was something odd about the way you kept hesitating, as if you didn't quite know what to do or where to go.'

She shrugged. 'I wasn't aware of being followed by someone who regretted not being invited to a barbecue.'

'I was invited,' he said. 'But it isn't my scene living it up with a crowd of teenagers. It's bad enough dealing with one sometimes, though Danny's a great help on occasions with my caretaking of the Mill.'

'You're the caretaker?'

'Until the affairs of my late great-uncle are finally sorted out. The house is not habitable, as you saw, but there's a chalet at the back large enough for us and a live-in housekeeper as a temporary measure.'

'She doesn't mind the loneliness of the place?'

'Not a bit. Mrs Barnes is in her seventies now, but happy to help out. Says she's too old to go gadding about.'

Alice smiled. 'You're lucky, then.'

'Not for long. She's off to live with her sister in Newbury as soon as the business at the Mill is settled. If it ever is. It's been going on for years. Something has to be done soon, but it could go either way.'

He stared down at his hands clasped in his lap. She knew Oakley Mill meant a great deal to him, and by the stern line of his jaw she could see that he was deeply worried. She wondered how successful his business really was, if he couldn't expand as he wished until he found larger premises than at Natalie's place.

She moved a little in her seat on the rock.

'Cold?' he said. 'Would you like to move on?'

She shook her head. 'Not just yet.'

'You have your worries too.'

She nodded. 'My grandfather would hate to think his death was the cause of them,' she said quietly.

'But you have to give yourself time to grieve.'

'I know that.'

'Don't try and do too much for the next few weeks, Alice. Natalie was anxious about you planning to go into business with Torville Satterly so soon.'

'She told you *that*?'

'Is it meant to be a secret?'

Alice felt herself flush, and for a moment was too taken aback to speak.

Tom seemed to notice nothing. 'I understand Natalie's concern,' he said.

'That chap's an exuberant character, full of energy, and might well try to push you into decisions you could later regret.'

'No-one would be able to do that,' Alice managed to get out.

'So why not let it rest for a week or two?'

'But . . . ' Alice began and then broke off, struggling to keep her composure.

'Natalie just wants to help.'

'*Help?* How can someone like Natalie help when she knows nothing about it?'

'More than you think, perhaps.'

'It's a pack of lies.'

'You mean it's not true?'

'True?' Alice sprang up. 'How can you even think it? Megan and I are a partnership and *Love-in-a-Mist* belongs to us. Why should Natalie think otherwise, unless she . . . '

Tom got up too and caught hold of her arms to steady her. 'Careful, or you'll be over the side.'

She tried to break free but his grip was firm.

'You're overreacting,' he said. 'Calm down, Alice.'

Alice gave a choking laugh. Her reaction would be nothing to Megan's when she heard of this.

Suddenly, she went limp in his hands in an effort to make him release her, but it made no difference. His arm was round her now, supporting her. She allowed a moment to pass, and then took a deep, trembling breath. 'Please let me go.'

'You're unwell . . . '

'I'm just angry at that woman's lies.'

'A mistake, obviously, nothing more.'

'I'm perfectly all right.'

She could tell he didn't believe her, because although he loosened his grip he still held on to one arm. She wished to be free of him, but at the same time his concern was balm to her shattered spirits.

'We don't need anyone else, Megan and me,' she stuttered. 'How can you think we would . . . And never Torville Satterly. What interest could a man like that possibly have in a place like ours? It's ridiculous.'

'He might have a good reason.'

'Such as?'

'He might care for one of the partners.'

She twisted round to glare at him but his face was inscrutable.

'You believe that?'

'I think Natalie does.'

'*Natalie*.'

'She's a helpful person, Alice. She has to be, in her job.'

'But this isn't her job.'

'A mistake, that's all. You're being unreasonable. You're overtired. You need to take things easy. Your friend should have seen that you did just that, instead of expecting you to work all hours. Be sensible, Alice.'

She gave a cry of rage, pulled her arm away from him and ran.

12

In the days that followed, Alice found a measure of comfort in the routine that had been established from the first. She thrust Tom's interference to the back of her mind on Monday as she got ready to accompany Megan on her weekly shopping expedition to Axminster, stocking up for her cooking and baking sessions that had become so popular that she now had a waiting list. Alice always enjoyed discussing menus on the way home when they stopped at some new place for lunch — and also for Megan to suss out the opposition and pick up as many tips as she could.

But today, Megan rang to say she wasn't feeling too good, and would Alice mind doing the shopping on her own?

This was disturbing and Alice said nothing for a moment.

'Alice, are you still there?'

'You're not pulling a fast one just to get out of it?'

'As if I would!'

'You'll have to give me a list, then.'

'I'll read it out.'

Alice flicked open the pad she kept by the phone. She jotted down a few items and then said, 'Why am I doing this when I could call in on my way and check how you are? Is Harry there?'

'Gone off to work, the lucky lad. It'll be great to see you, Alice my friend, but I'm all right; just feel a bit tired and weak, that's all.'

This was unlike her friend, and Alice hurried to find her bag, change her shoes and be off. Ten minutes later she drove through the wide gateway of Rose Lodge, and drew up outside the open front door.

'Megan?'

'Come on through. I'm in the conservatory.'

She was lying on the wicker sofa, and looked so pale that Alice was alarmed.

Megan laughed and sat up. 'Don't look like that, Alice. I'm not at death's door.'

'You could have fooled me.'

'It'll pass in its own good time, so they tell me. Oh Alice, I'm so excited.'

'Excited? About what?' But as soon as the words were out of her mouth, Alice knew the reason. 'You don't mean . . . ?'

'I am, oh, I am. Isn't it wonderful?'

A rush of warm tears filled Alice's eyes as she rushed to her friend and gave her a hug. 'Is it really true?'

'I wanted to tell you, but not over the phone. A baby of our own! Harry is simply thrilled.'

'And so am I, dear Megan.'

'After all this time.'

'When is it due?'

'About Christmas time. Won't it be perfect?'

Alice was glad to rejoice with her, knowing that this was not the time to tell Megan about Natalie Tanner's odd remark.

'We need to celebrate,' said Megan, her face alight with happiness.

'That's for you and Harry to do.'

'And you and me too. Why not? Two celebrations are better than one. As soon as this morning sickness passes, I'll be up for something special, Alice.'

Alice smiled. 'If you say so. Meanwhile you obviously need to rest.'

'Too much to do. So much to plan.'

'Like cancelling your baking classes?'

'No way.'

'But how can you cope with them, feeling as you do? And there's the lunch you do on Wednesdays and Saturdays for my workshop people. I could sort something out there, of course. No problem. But it's your baking classes that will be difficult.'

Megan smiled. 'Harry came up with the perfect solution until this sickness thing has passed. I'll put the time of the classes back a bit; I'm always all right in the afternoons. I'll get them to come at twelve. We'll have a bit of a talk and demo first, then a simple lunch of filled baguettes or something. After that, we'll get stuck in with some hands-on baking and so on during the afternoon, and they can take the results home at teatime.'

'But what about the cream teas?'

Megan's face clouded and then cleared again. 'I'd forgotten that. But, wait a minute, how long does it take to knock up a few scones? The garden gate will be open and the notice on it in place. People can come in that way and find seats, and you'll be there as well, won't you Alice, to welcome them?'

'Of course.'

'They won't come if it's raining. It's the view they like, and the garden. But if they do, we can accommodate them inside. We can do it.'

Alice considered. 'It could work.'

'It will,' Megan said with confidence. 'Danny'll be pleased. My lot will still be here when he finishes afternoon school and he can join us.'

'In time for the clearing up?'

'In time for a bit of a feast of

whatever we've been doing.'

'You've got it all planned. But what about when the baby's born?'

'We'll deal with that when the time comes,' Megan said airily.

'If you say so,' Alice said. Her friend was on such a high that she was glad to sit here and let her talk, and by the time she stood up to go shopping, some colour had returned to Megan's cheeks and her eyes were bright.

On the way back to Lyme with a loaded car, Alice couldn't help thinking that, now Megan's attention would be on her pregnancy — as it should be — poor *Love-in-a-Mist* must take second place. But at least for the moment they could continue with the cream teas, which were turning out to be good financially. Had Megan been fully fit they could have started having them on her workshop days, as they had been had been considering.

But whatever Megan said, once the baby was born things would have to change. They would have to think this through very carefully, and a different sort of plan would need to be worked out for the future. If there *was* a future for them at *Love-in-a-Mist* after Natalie's attempts to jeopardise it.

But they were good at plans, and Megan liked a challenge.

★ ★ ★

On Wednesday there was a sombre mood among some of the members of the workshop group as they came in from the cold greyness outside and set up their easels.

'Call this summer?' one of them grumbled.

'It's warm in here, Monica,' an elderly man said cheerfully.

'But for how much longer?' Monica said.

Alice looked at her in surprise. Megan's pregnancy couldn't be common knowledge already, surely? 'What d'you mean?'

'I heard you're moving on, Alice, and closing this place down.'

'Me? No, you've got that wrong.'

'Are you sure?'

There was a murmuring from some of the others.

'I think I'd be the first to know, don't you?' Alice said.

Monica was still not convinced. 'I felt sure you'd be telling us today.'

Alice shrugged as she helped move a table in to a better position. 'So who is this mystery person who knows more about my intentions than I do myself?'

'I heard that you'd injured your wrist, Alice,' someone else volunteered.

Alice waggled both of them in the air. 'Does either of them look injured?'

'A miraculous recovery in the nick of time?' Peter suggested, sitting down heavily in his chair. He had arranged his giant acrylic tubes in neat rows in front of him and looked all ready to begin.

Alice laughed, although she wasn't really amused. 'Do you think I should put an announcement in the *Lyme Advertiser* to say that I'm in perfect health with no bodily injuries, and have no intention of moving anywhere?'

'It might help,' said Monica doubtfully. 'I heard it in the butcher's, too.'

'Help me, someone,' Alice begged. 'Tell me who started this.'

'You first heard it from that nice girl in the Holiday Team place, didn't you, Monica?' Peter said. 'The one with fair sleek hair, always smiling.'

'You know her, Alice?'

Alice nodded. This sounded serious. It seemed that Natalie Tanner had definitely been at work intending to do them harm. She tapped her fingers on the table in front of her, wondering was best to do about it. 'Believe me, none of this is true,' she said.

'So, business isn't as bad as they say, then?'

'And you and Megan haven't had a blazing row?'

'You're not running off with that lovely Torville?'

'Oh, *please*!'

'We believe you.'

'Of course we do, Alice.'

'And you'll scotch any silly rumours you come across?'

There was a murmur of support, and for the moment Alice felt she could breathe again. Surely no-one who knew her and Megan would believe such things? But some of the members of this group obviously had had doubts.

At least there was a lightening of the atmosphere now. Several people were planning to use the sketches they had done the other day on the river bank to inspire their paintings, most of them using oils or acrylics. As Alice moved among them offering suggestions, she couldn't help thinking that she would have to put a stop to these rumours somehow. But how could you stop them once they were floating about out there for anyone to pick up and pass on?

★　★　★

Megan was full of high spirits when she arrived to start the preparations for the

266

cream teas. 'I'm going to make the scones here today, seeing as you've stuffed the cupboard full of ingredients, Alice,' she said.

'Only on your orders.'

'Let me get at them. And then I'll get the tables out.'

'You're planning to set up outside?'

'Why not?'

'Because it's grey and miserable-looking,' said Alice. 'Because it might rain.' *And because no-one might come if they think we're shutting down.* She didn't voice the last reason, of course, in case Megan's blood pressure shot sky-high.

'Rubbish,' said Megan. 'I saw a bit of blue sky on the way here.'

'Always the optimist.'

'It looks good to have the tables out there, anyway.'

Alice smiled, glad to see that Megan looked a lot better than when she had last seen her. What did a few tables outside matter, even if no-one used them because they preferred to be indoors? If they came at all.

'I'm not sure serving the cream teas every day is a good idea after all,' she said.

'Worth a try,' said Megan. 'It makes sense not to miss out on every opportunity, as we said. I'm full of energy now.'

'It's tough on you, Megan.'

Megan shrugged as she reached for her apron. 'So how did the lunch for your lot go?' she asked as Alice was about to return to the workshop group in the other room.

'Fine. I kept it simple and no-one minded. The chocolate cheesecake cake helped. They loved it. Thanks for getting Harry to bring it in. And the salad platter was a godsend.'

'The least I could do,' said Megan, already busy with the rolling pin. 'As soon as these are in the oven, I'll get outside and sort those tables out. It's all right, they're light enough for me to carry. You get back to your duties.'

The clouds had cleared and the sun

was shining by the time the workshop drew to a close. Several people from the workshop decided to stay for a cream tea today, and others joined them. As soon as Danny arrived, Alice slipped away, saying she had something to do in town and wouldn't be long.

She found Natalie in a small room that did duty as an office at the back of the building where the Tourist Team worked. The bigger room, devoid of customers, felt eerily bleak, even though the walls were decorated with colourful posters advertising the joys of Lyme and featuring lurid blue sea and yellow sand such as she had never seen. Perhaps it was the high ceiling and curtainless windows with the view of stone walls that gave it an austere atmosphere, Alice thought.

Natalie was sorting papers at her desk. She sprang up immediately and ran her hands down her long, dark skirt as if she needed to brush something away. 'Can I help you?'

'That depends,' said Alice.

Natalie's smile didn't quite reach her eyes. 'On what?'

'Someone is spreading untrue rumours about me. You wouldn't happen to know who that person could possibly be?'

'Why should anyone want to do that?'

'Let's see ... to harm *Love-in-a-Mist*; to gain favour with someone like Tom Carey; for a bit of a laugh. What do you think?'

'Why are you asking me?' Natalie's hand flew to her hair, and she smoothed it back although not a hair was out of place.

'Why indeed?'

'So you're accusing me.'

'Is there any good reason why I shouldn't?'

'You can't prove anything.'

'No?'

There was silence between them as Alice waited for the retort she felt sure was coming. But Natalie hesitated, seemed about to speak, and then was silent.

'Just make sure you put an end to these lies at once,' said Alice at last. 'You're a member of the Tourist Team. A professional. It wouldn't look good to be sued for setting out to hurt a new business in the town by passing on vicious rumours. Or even starting them. Think about it.'

Natalie cleared her throat and seemed to gain strength from it. 'There's no smoke without fire,' she said crisply. 'Your good friend, Torville Satterly, was in here the other day, extolling your virtues and ranting on about Beer. Others heard him too. Who knows what conclusions they may have drawn?'

Alice gave a dry laugh. 'Who knows? But they wouldn't be the same as the ones you've been asserting, I'll bet. And maybe the fire you mentioned burned a little brighter fanned by comments from you?'

'I don't think so.' Natalie shrugged and sat down in a purposeful way. 'And now I've work to do. We've a busy

271

schedule ahead.'

'Me too,' said Alice. 'And please see to it that these rumours stop.'

Natalie said nothing and Alice turned to leave, knowing she could do no more for the moment, but feeling better for having tried.

She drew Danny to one side when she got back to *Love-in-a-Mist* and explained the situation to him.

'And you think Natalie is behind it,' he said, round-eyed.

'And don't spread that about,' she said sharply. 'I don't want Megan to know anything about it either.'

'I'd fight Natalie if I were you,' he said. 'Shall I do it for you?'

'Definitely not.'

He looked disappointed, and she hastened to give him a job collecting up the jam dishes and dealing with the leftover contents.

'I could fill Natalie's place with fossils,' he said when that was done.

'Are you mad?'

'It would really annoy her. She hates

them. I wouldn't use real ones, of course. It would be a waste. I'd bring lots of rocks back from the beach and pretend there were hidden fossils in them. There's no room for them in Tom's workshop, so I'll stack them in her hall. Then she'll be sure to trip over them and break her leg.'

Alice smiled. 'Stop fantasising and get off home.'

He sighed. 'You're no fun at all. Don't you like fossils?'

'Love them,' said Alice promptly.

'I reckon you should have some here in the window. Why don't you come with me one day on a fossil hunt?'

'Maybe one day,' said Alice. 'And now you really must go, Danny. Tom will be waiting for you.' A thought suddenly struck her. 'Danny . . . you said there was no room in Tom's workshop for the fossils or whatever. Where *is* his workshop?'

'Don't you know?'

'Would I be asking if I did?'

'S'pose not.'

'So where is it then?'

'It's a rickety old outbuilding. It's the best he could get.'

'And?'

'At Natalie's place. I've got to meet him there.'

'Then get along there, why don't you?'

He went and she watched him go, deep in thought.

★　★　★

'I've been hearing things,' said Torville as he lowered himself into one of the chairs in the garden of *Love-in-a-Mist* on Saturday afternoon.

'What things?' said Megan, standing poised with pad and pencil to take his order.

'A double cream tea, please, if you will.'

'Double? You're expecting someone to join you?'

His eyes gleamed at her. 'I'd ask you, my dear, if you weren't so busy running back and forth wearing a frilly apron. A pretty one, I must say. Is it your best?'

'And Alice is busy too,' Megan said tightly.

'Ah yes, dear Alice.' Torville sighed. 'I admit it's Alice I've come to see.'

'And why aren't I surprised?'

'I shall wait until her workshop is finished. I shall eat my two cream teas.'

'You're crazy.'

'And I'll enjoy every mouthful.'

Megan scribbled something on her pad, smiled briefly and departed. Later, as she checked the big room when the last of Alice's group were departing, she took a quick look out of the window.

'What's the matter?' Alice said.

'Torville's out there.'

'So are a lot of people. You're doing well. I'll come and help in a minute.'

'He's in a funny mood. He's been there for at least an hour. He'll burst if he eats much more.'

'Good for business, though.'

'Be serious, Alice.'

Alice sighed. 'I'm being serious.' It

seemed that people had come this afternoon out of curiosity, to suss out these rumours for themselves, and although she was glad to see them she didn't like thinking of the possible reason.

'He says he won't go until he has spoken to you.'

'Then I'd better go out to him.'

She found him at the far table, flicking a paper napkin at Pickles who obviously thought it was some sort of game. Torville turned a flushed face to her as she walked across the grass. 'Please call this animal off.'

She smiled and made a grab for the cat. 'He thinks you're playing with him, Torville, that's all.'

'Playing!' he said in disgust.

Pickles had lost interest now, and didn't like being snatched up in such an undignified way. He struggled for freedom and Alice let him go.

She sat down at the table. 'You wanted to speak to me, Torville?'

'To speak *with* you, my dear. What is

this I hear about you giving up here and coming to be with me in Beer?'

She sat down opposite him and looked at him in dismay. 'You've heard that too?'

'It's all round town.'

'Torville, it's simply not true.'

'The giving up here, or coming with me?'

He looked at her so kindly that she felt tears spring to her eyes. She reached for a spare napkin and rubbed at them.

'So someone's been starting bad rumours?' he said.

She nodded.

'Who is this someone?'

'She won't admit it and we've got no proof.'

'But you know who it was?'

'She wants something she thinks I have. Someone.'

'Someone? And how does this someone feel about her?'

Alice looked him helplessly. 'I don't know.'

'And she'll ruin your reputation for that?'

'And yours too, Torville.'

He leaned forward. 'She won't ruin mine. It's an honour for me to know that someone thinks you might care enough for me to do just that.'

'Or she pretends to think it.'

He sank back in his chair and was still for a moment sitting with his eyes closed. Alice gazed at him, understanding for the first time that his feelings beneath his show of eccentricity ran deeper than she had imagined and she felt humbled by the knowledge.

'Are you really relocating to Beer?' she said gently.

He opened his eyes. 'You will always be in my heart, Alice,' he said. 'My dear, I know I'm not for you, but I care enough for you to want to put an end to this worry once and for all. I shall confront her on your behalf, putting a few things before her. She'll find the lease on her cottage likely to run out if she is not very careful.'

'How do you know?'

He tapped the side of his nose. 'Trust me.' He struggled to his feet. 'I see that most of your customers have gone, and I mustn't linger either. Your friend's on edge, I expect, waiting for me to pay the bill. Look after yourself, Alice. Come to Beer sometimes to view my ongoing exhibitions, in a charming place I've been introduced to by someone not a million miles from here.'

He had surprised her into silence.

He smiled and patted her on the shoulder. 'Goodbye, my dear. And be happy.'

13

The metal moorhens on the patch of grass bordering the millstream at Oakley looked so realistic from a distance that Alice could almost believe they were real. She drove along the rutted track to the mill and parked in her usual place. Nearby, some rabbits and several storks lurked in the long grass; and across the way were three beautiful swans that, had they been white, would have startled her even more than they did with their exquisite design and beauty.

The real geese came clacking towards her as Alice removed three canvasses from her car and made her way over to Martin's framing workshop.

'I know you're real because of the racket you're making,' she told them. 'You can't fool me.'

The leader gave one last ferocious

hiss and then retreated to join the others, who had already given up and were wandering away.

By the workshop door, a group of frogs lingered, along with several hedgehogs.

'So what are they all doing here?' she said as she went inside.

Martin looked up from his workshop and smiled. 'Wasted here, aren't they, with no one much to see and appreciate them?'

'But why are they here?'

'Tom's doing a bit of stocktaking.'

'They're works of art,' said Alice. 'Especially seeing them here in a natural habitat.' She thought of the moorhens around the pretend pond in the window of the *Pool of Dreams* that she and Megan had admired, and wondered now how Olivia and her brother were faring. With Torville Satterly on their case, everything might have changed for the better. Or worse. She smiled as she imagined Torville taking over, booming out his instructions and filling the place with his huge personality.

'You know he's leaving?'

'Tom?'

Martin shrugged as he wiped his hands on a cloth and came forward to the counter. 'He deserves better, but it seems hopeless; there's no suitable property available in the area for him to expand and get his business off the ground.'

Alice said nothing as she unwrapped her paintings and laid them out for Martin to see. He looked carefully at the first, and then selected a sample from the selection on the board. As he held it in position for her to see, he said, 'He was in here yesterday, poor chap, trying to come to some sort of decision. There's the boy's schooling to think about, of course, though it's not too certain what will be happening there.'

'I know Danny is happy at the local school.'

'The problem is that things have come to a head sooner than Tom thought, and there's nowhere suitable for the space he needs in Lyme.'

Except *Love-in-a-Mist* at a pinch, Alice thought. She smoothed her finger along the piece of wood Martin had selected. 'This looks good,' she said. 'But wider, I think. Could we try it?'

'Why not?'

But she could see at once that it wouldn't do. She frowned. 'Does that mean Tom will have to move right away?'

'We could try a lighter colour if you like. This one?'

She shook her head. 'I think you were right first time.'

'As you wish.' He wrote the measurements down, consulted his list and mentioned a price.

That done, she chose suitable wood with which to frame the other two paintings, thinking all the while about Tom.

'His work is good, don't you think?' Martin said as he finished his calculations and moved the paintings one at a time to his workbench. 'I can have these ready for you in two or three days,' he said.

'Thank you. I wondered why so many of his animals and birds had been brought here.'

'Nowhere else to put them since he's had notice to quit. Not that the place at Western Beach was ideal, but it was better than nothing.'

'Western Cottage?' she said in surprise. *Natalie's place?*

'He needed to be somewhere in Lyme, and was glad to be there on a temporary basis. But now that's not possible.'

'I see.'

What had Torville been up to? Alice felt an icy chill.

'There was somewhere down near Land's End he went to look at yesterday, I believe.'

'So far away.'

'It can't be helped. But I shall miss him.'

Me too, she thought with a pang. It

was indirectly because of her that this had arisen in the first place, and now they were likely to lose Danny as well.

Instead of getting into the car and driving back to *Love-in-a-Mist*, she walked across the grass to the large pond where the ducks had their home. Today they had gone wandering off elsewhere. She almost expected to see metal moorhens clustered here too, but there was nothing,

She stood for a moment and looked about her, at the old mill buildings that were almost ruined now. Then she set off to walk round the edge of the water, watching the ripples move across from one bank to the other in the vagaries of the breeze. Apart from that slight feel of movement in the air, there was no sound, and the silence rang in her ears. She felt empty, bereft.

Tom was going, Danny too, and there was nothing she could do about it if she didn't give up the lease of *Love-in-a-Mist* to him. And how could she do that with Megan to consider?

She sat for a while on a fallen log, at the edge of the grove of trees that edged one side of the pond, and gazed at the water. She ached to see Tom, but dreaded it too, because she would see in his face his determination to start afresh in some other place of which she knew nothing.

★　★　★

It was windier down in Lyme, and when Danny came in after school, full of excitement, his curly hair was ruffled and his cheeks pink.

'We're moving,' he said.

'All of you?'

He nodded, brimming with excitement. 'I came to tell you.'

Alice straightened one of her new paintings she had placed on an easel near the window, and stood back to see how it looked. 'So you won't be helping Megan out for much longer?' she said.

For a moment Danny looked sad. 'Will she miss me?'

'Of course. Me too.'

'Tom's looking for somewhere. He can't go searching tomorrow, because there's an important meeting somewhere he wouldn't tell me about, and there's an even more important one on Sunday. So he's gone today and he could be late back. Can I stay here till he comes?'

'He's gone with Natalie?'

'Why her?'

'Haven't they gone looking together?'

Danny looked uncertain. 'I didn't think of that.'

Alice had thought of nothing else since she had got back from Oakley Mill, and now she wasn't at all sure she wanted to see them together. In fact, she knew she didn't. 'What arrangement did Tom make to pick you up?' she said.

'Down by the harbour at six o'clock.'

'It's nearly that now.'

'He'll know where I am.'

'Not good enough,' she said.

'Oh, all right,' he said grudgingly.

'I'll walk part of the way down with you, and we can talk about the fossil-searching expedition you invited me to. Is it still on? The sooner we do it the better, if you're clearing off, but you'd better keep Tom in the picture.'

'You're on,' he said. 'Tomorrow?'

'Sunday,' she said. 'I'll see you down on the beach.'

'Will ten o'clock do? Martin is sure to bring me in if I ask him. He comes to Lyme every Sunday just a bit before ten o'clock, to see his friend and go to church with her, so that's good.'

'Then ten o'clock it is,' she said.

She left him near the bottom of the hill.

* * *

By Saturday afternoon the wind had risen dramatically, banging shut the door into the back garden almost before Alice had time to let an infuriated Pickles inside. Most of the workshop group decided to pack up early, until

288

only Suzie and Brian and a temporary member, a geology student from Bristol University staying with his parents in the town during the summer, were left.

His painting in oil bars was of the cliffs in a storm such as was threatening to develop outside, with black clouds towering over everything.

Alice shivered as she looked at it. 'You've caught the atmosphere perfectly, Kevin,' she said.

He grinned, tossing his ginger head and looking like a naughty schoolboy. 'D'you think I'm going to make it happen?'

'I hope not. It's bad for business, you know.'

Megan had given up on the cream teas as a bad job, and after hanging around for a bit in case anyone turned up in this weather, she left for home. Danny, though, was still here, his nose pressed against the windowpane, looking out over the windswept garden to the heaving waves in the bay.

'Your work looks impressive, Kevin,'

Suzie said, looking up from her delicate watercolour painting of pink roses in a blue bowl.

Kevin was too engrossed in what he was doing to answer. Alice was glad he had joined them, as he brought a breath of enthusiasm into the group that was good for them all.

At last, the three of them were ready to go.

'Can I give you a lift anywhere, Kevin?' Brian asked. 'I'm bringing the car to the door to get this lady settled into it, and you're welcome to come too.' He glanced at Danny. 'What about you, young man? Have you far to go?'

Danny shrugged. 'Oakley Mill.'

'*Oakley* Mill?' Brian looked surprised.

'I live there,' said Danny. 'In a chalet at the back. One day I want to live in the mill full-time.'

Brian smiled. 'No problem, Danny. It's on our way.'

Danny looked at Alice for confirmation, and she nodded. 'Will Tom be there?' she asked.

'Someone will. Thanks. I'd like a lift.'

'Off you go, then.'

Alice watched them leave, wondering who the someone was. But she mustn't think of that now. She had work to do here, tidying the place up, and she must concentrate her thoughts on that.

Easier said than done, of course. She wished now that she had suggested Danny wait for Tom here, and contact him on his mobile to tell him. That way, she could see Tom again, if only for a short time. The way things were happening, that might be difficult in the days ahead.

But what could she say to him, apart from wishing him good luck wherever he chose to settle? And then a painful parting.

★　★　★

The wind rose even more during the night, whipping round the building and rattling the glass in the windows. Alice slept fitfully, jerking awake every now and again after dreams of falling masonry. The rain came just before dawn, soaking the grass in seconds, but by the time Alice was at the door, trying to persuade the reluctant Pickles that he really wanted a stroll outside, it had stopped.

As she stood waiting for him to return, she saw that one of the branches of the sycamore in the garden bordering theirs had come down, half-lying across the adjoining hedge. But at least the wind was easing now.

She switched on the radio to listen to the local news while eating her cereal. Pickles, happy now, was lapping water in a satisfying sort of way. The serious tone of the newsreader alerted her, and she lifted her head to listen to reports of a cliff-fall at Lyme during the night.

'The public are warned to keep away for their own safety,' the newscaster said.

Danny?

Alice glanced at her watch and leapt

up, her cereal spoon clattering to the floor. Surely he would have had the sense to keep clear? Though Danny revelled in challenges, happily taking part in activities in which he saw no danger. Martin could have heard the news, and told Danny there was nothing doing today in the way of fossil-hunting — for him or anyone else. But how could she be sure of that? She couldn't, and her imagination was running riot. For her peace of mind, there was nothing for it but to run down to Western Beach and check Danny was keeping clear.

She grabbed her jacket and thrust her feet into the boots she kept for gardening. At the bottom of the hill that lead down to Western Beach, a crowd had already gathered. She joined them, her eyes scanning the people.

'I'm looking for someone,' she said, her mouth dry.

She slipped past them unnoticed, and crunched her way across the shingle to the cliffs. She saw the fall of rocks and earth ahead of her but couldn't see anyone searching there for those fossils Danny was so keen on collecting.

Behind her, she heard a shout, and the sound of running feet.

'Alice. *Alice!*'

She swung round.

'Wait!'

Then Danny was with her, almost too breathless to speak. 'We're not allowed to be here,' he gasped out.

She saw that there was someone following him, her face suffused with anger.

'You fool, Danny,' Natalie screamed. 'Get back at once.'

'But I couldn't. Alice . . . '

'Do as I say!' She slapped him hard on the cheek.

Astonished, he stared at her. His hand flew to his face.

'What are you doing?' Alice cried.

Natalie shot her a look of such hatred that for a moment Alice thought she would be attacked too.

And then Tom was with them. 'That's enough, Natalie!'

'But I was only trying to help.'

Ignoring her, he grabbed hold of Alice. 'What are you doing, Alice? I was worried sick. Have you no sense?'

Suddenly, she had no strength to do anything but droop there in front of him. The beach and cliffs were a dazzling whirl, and the roaring in her ears was like thunder. A moment later, she felt herself fall, and then she was lying on the hard shingle with Tom bending over her.

'Alice?'

She closed her eyes.

'*Alice?*'

She shuddered and opened them again, and saw him through swirling mist.

'Are you all right?' said Danny's voice, deeply anxious. 'Shall I phone for an ambulance?'

'*No!*' The mist was gradually clearing now and Alice struggled to sit up.

'Keep still.'

'I'm all right, Tom.'

'Do as I say,' he ordered, his voice steely.

But she had no sense any more. She managed to get to her feet. 'Please, don't fuss.'

'Fuss? You were doing something stupid, and you tell me not to fuss?' He sounded really angry now.

'I was looking for Danny. I thought he was here.'

Tom glanced at his watch. 'I'm late. I'll have to go.'

'You can take your belongings with you,' Natalie cried. 'If you don't, I'll dump the lot of them outside.'

'My plans exactly after what you've just done.' Tom's face was pale and there was such a stern look about his mouth that Alice was alarmed.

'I never want to see you again.' Natalie's bitter words seemed to hang in the air in the momentary silence that followed. Then she turned and ran.

'I'll look after Alice,' said Danny.

'I don't like to leave you, but I must,' Tom said, his face taut. 'Get Alice to the nearest café for a hot drink, Danny. Here, take this.'

And then he was gone.

'He had to go,' said Danny as they watched him stride across the shingle. 'We'd better go too, Alice. Can you walk?'

'I think so. I know so.'

They walked slowly to the kiosk a little way along the road that backed onto the beach, passing Western Cottage on the way.

Danny barely gave it a glance, but Alice had a quick look to see if Natalie had carried out her threat and piled Tom's belongings outside her door. She hadn't.

'Don't bother with *her*,' said Danny. 'Tom's already moved most of his stuff, and I don't suppose the rest matters much.'

'Tom knew this was coming?'

Danny shrugged. 'Who knows?'

He ordered two giant coffees and two lots of toasted cheese sandwiches.

'You're not hungry, by any chance?' said Alice.

'I won't be when I've eaten my share of those.'

Alice knew that she wouldn't be, either.

'So how long will Tom be?' she asked as they sat on a low wall and prepared to eat. 'You'd better come back to *Love-in-a-Mist* with me, hadn't you?'

'Is Megan there?'

'Not on a Sunday.'

'Tom wants to ask her if she'll give me private cooking lessons,' he said. 'Do you think she would?'

'He'll have to ask her.'

He took an exploratory bite of his sandwich and found it was cool enough to eat. He took another mouthful. 'He thinks she's a bit fierce sometimes, but that's all to the good when there are difficult people to deal with.'

'Who had he in mind?'

Danny shrugged. 'How should I know?'

Alice could think of one at least, but Tom seemed to have done a good job with Natalie Tanner himself, and it was unlikely she would come near Megan again.

'So, *Love-in-a-Mist* it is, until Tom gets back?'

'If you want.'

'Here, you'd better have half of my sandwich, Danny. I can't eat it all.' Carefully, Alice broke it in two and handed a piece to him.

'Thanks.' Danny finished eating and wiped his mouth with his hand. 'If Tom's back too soon, it's bad news. The meeting is really important, but he thinks he'll be too late now.'

'Too late?' said Alice.

Danny frowned. 'He had to be there to sign things on the dot if he wanted everything to go through.'

Her blood seemed to leave her body and to flow back icy-cold. 'This is about Oakley Mill?'

'He came here to collect me when he heard about the cliff fall. He'd have had time, but he saw you and thought you were in danger . . . '

She was horrified. 'Because of me, he was held up?'

'We'll know when he gets back.'

With a heavy heart, Alice drank the rest of her coffee, and then they walked up to *Love-in-a-Mist*.

Tom was a good man, she thought, wanting to do the best for the boy in his care. She had never given Tom the credit he deserved; and now, through her, he was likely to be in danger of missing a meeting that was important to him.

14

Megan replaced the phone on the receiver on the bedside table and turned to look at Harry in bed beside her. 'Olivia knows it's short notice, but would we like to go over to *Pool of Dreams* for a special Sunday lunch?'

'Sunday lunch?' said Harry, as if he had never heard of such a thing.

'She'll be asking Alice too. She's got something to show us.'

'It had better be good.'

'It's a celebration of some sort. Do let's go, Harry.'

'If you feel up to it.'

Megan laughed. 'I've never felt so well in all my life.' To prove it she swung her legs out of bed and stood up. 'Wait a minute, though.'

'What now?'

'What time is it?'

'Nearly ten o'clock.'

'She won't get through to Alice. She's fossil-hunting with Danny this morning. What a shame. I'd better tell Olivia. Her number's in the book downstairs.'

'What's wrong with dialling 1471?'

'What would I do without you, my love?' Megan sat down on the bed and reached across for the phone. Moments later, holding her hand over the mouthpiece, she looked at Harry in alarm. 'There's been a cliff-fall down in Lyme in the night,' she said. 'You don't think . . . ?'

'Alice has more sense than that.'

'But has Danny?'

'Phone Alice on her mobile to find out.'

Megan blew him a kiss and spoke into her phone again. 'I'll get back to you, Olivia. Give me a minute or two. What shall I tell Alice?'

'Tell her my news can wait,' said Olivia's clear voice at the other end. 'It's about Torville making lots of changes at *Pool of Dreams*. He's made such a difference to the place. I love him!'

'You don't mean that?'

Olivia's voice softened. 'I think I do. He thinks so too.'

Megan turned to smile at Harry as she clicked on Alice's number. 'Alice will be surprised when I tell her.'

'Don't forget to warn her of further cliff-falls.'

'Alice won't need that.'

But Alice wasn't answering, and Megan left a message on voicemail. 'She'll be with Danny, making sure he's OK,' she said. Then she phoned Olivia again. She had some good news to tell her too, but that could wait.

★ ★ ★

It was over an hour before Tom came. Alice was showing Danny how to make scones in her kitchen upstairs. As the bell rang, Danny, flushed with triumph, was lifting the baking tray out of the oven.

She ran down to let Tom in and to invite him to join them. She could see at once from his broad smile and glittering eyes that he was triumphant, too. Her relief was enormous, and for a moment she couldn't speak.

'How are you now, Alice?'

'Fine, thanks.' She felt herself flush at his intent look as if he could see deep into her innermost being.

'Danny's not been bothering you?'

She smiled. 'Does he look as if he's a bother?'

'Come on then, you two,' he said. 'Leave everything. We'll pick up a takeaway and eat at Oakley Mill.'

'I'll bring my scones,' said Danny.

Alice produced a container, checked the oven was switched off, and followed the others downstairs and out to Tom's car.

He drove swiftly, saying nothing more until they had negotiated the bumpy track and he pulled up near the waterwheel.

They got out.

'Right, Danny,' he said. 'How about tidying up the chalet to make it fit for Alice to see? Then we've plans to make.'

'Permanent ones?' said Danny hopefully.

Tom ruffled Danny's curly hair. 'Definitely permanent. All's well, Danny. We have something to celebrate.'

'That's good,' said Danny. 'See you!'

For a moment Tom gazed at the waterwheel as if he couldn't see enough. 'I'll be able to start work on that soon to get it going again,' he said. 'I'll look into what grants are available.'

'So it's good news?'

'Come and see.'

He ushered her into the barn-like building that was partly over the waterwheel, and in the musty gloom she saw the remains of several floors above where they were standing. Part of a staircase was there, and some of the beams looked solid enough, but the whole effect was one of desolation at first glance, even though Tom radiated enthusiasm.

'There's a lot to be done, of course,' he said, his voice vibrant.

For a moment, it seemed to her impossible that it could ever be restored; but then, standing there at his side, she began to imagine it as it had once been when the waterwheel was turning. She could almost hear the creak of machinery.

He turned to her. 'You see it too?'

She nodded.

'There's more.'

He led her outside again, and she blinked in the sudden light as the sun emerged from a bank of cloud. As if on cue, the geese appeared, hissing a welcome. They stayed for a moment, and then, uncaring, went about their business.

'Your moorhens and other things have all gone,' Alice said.

'They're packed up to fulfil orders,' he said. 'Now I shall be able to set up here and produce a lot more.'

'So it's all settled, then?'

'It's mine now, in trust for Danny.

There's a bit of money available at last towards the restoration work: interest-free loans, and so forth.'

She knew her eyes shone. 'That's wonderful, Tom.'

For a moment, he looked grim. 'For ages it seemed impossibly complicated. I needed to be nearby and to be able to carry on my metalwork. In the end it was dependent on my willingness to be Danny's legal guardian until he's eighteen. We both wanted it, of course. But other family members had to agree, and it all took far too long. It had to be the right decision.'

'Of course.'

'You believe it is, Alice?'

'Of course. Danny's a good scone-maker, and that's useful if you always forget the takeaways.'

He smiled. 'My mind was on other things. But no problem. I'll phone for a home delivery in a minute.'

'Home?'

'Let me show you the house.'

This was less of a ruin than the mill

building, but still in a state of disrepair. Old wallpaper hung in strips from the walls, and the glass in most of the downstairs windows was broken. She could see that the oak staircase had been beautiful in its day — and maybe, with plenty of loving attention, could be again. She ran her hands a little way up the banisters and found them covered in dust.

'Shall we go up? Be careful.'

The bedrooms smelt of neglect, but were as spacious as the rooms downstairs, and in far better condition. Gallons of hot water and a scrubbing brush would do wonders for the wooden floor, she thought. She went across to the fitted wardrobe in the alcove of the largest room, and pulled open the door. Inside was a row of drawers with shelves above as well as plenty of hanging space.

'Useful,' she said. 'This place will make a lovely home one day.'

He turned a radiant face to her. 'I'd like you to share it with me, Alice.'

She took a deep, gasping breath.

At once he was all contrition. 'I meant to wait. I meant to show you everything and tell you my plans for the immediate future, to get things underway here at Oakley first. And then to ask a question that means all the world to me, instead of blurting something out now like a fool.'

'Show me everything now,' she said.

She seemed to be walking on air as they went downstairs and out into the sunshine to look at the rest of the outbuildings, and for him to tell of the plans he was already considering for them. But she hardly listened to what he was saying because she was filled with such wondering joy.

He was offering her something that meant the world to him.

'There's a huge amount of space,' he said. 'Painting workshops could be held here. Would people come?'

'I think so. Handy for Martin's framing.'

Tom nodded. 'His business could well

expand. We could set up a restaurant, too, with someone like Megan in charge and others to help do the work.'

'Danny will be pleased.'

'Ah yes, Danny,' he said. 'It's worth thinking about.'

'With a little one on the way, I think Megan should give up her work at *Love-in-a-Mist*.'

He smiled. 'That's delightful news.'

'I'd need to think about *Love-in-a-Mist*.'

'A showroom for my work down in Lyme?'

She laughed. 'You were determined to have it.'

He laughed too. 'You should know I always get what I want, given time.'

'Like Danny.'

'And you, Alice, my darling girl.'

She gazed dreamily across the grass to the waterwheel. 'I think I'll sell my grandfather's cottage. It seems the right thing to do. Perhaps a young married couple will buy it and start a happy life there together.'

'Just as we shall start a happy life here,' he said. There was a soft expression in his eyes now. 'Alice, my dearest love, will you be my wife?'

He bent and kissed her and her body seemed to melt into his. And when he released her at last, she saw the love in his eyes that she knew was reflected in her own.

We do hope that you have enjoyed reading this large print book.

Did you know that all of our titles are available for purchase?

We publish a wide range of high quality large print books including:
Romances, Mysteries, Classics
General Fiction
Non Fiction and Westerns

Special interest titles available in large print are:
The Little Oxford Dictionary
Music Book, Song Book
Hymn Book, Service Book

Also available from us courtesy of Oxford University Press:
Young Readers' Dictionary
(large print edition)
Young Readers' Thesaurus
(large print edition)

For further information or a free brochure, please contact us at:
Ulverscroft Large Print Books Ltd.,
The Green, Bradgate Road, Anstey,
Leicester, LE7 7FU, England.
Tel: (00 44) 0116 236 4325
Fax: (00 44) 0116 234 0205

REGAN'S FALL

Valerie Holmes

After the death of their father and the removal of their gentle mother to debtors' prison, Regan and her brother Isaac are left in desperate circumstances. Their only hope is to appeal for aid from an estranged relative at Marram Hall, Lady Arianne, whom neither sibling has ever met. Upon her arrival, Regan encounters the handsome and masterful James Coldwell, the local magistrate, but fears that if she trusts him he will throw her and Isaac out of the house — or worse. Then Lady Arianne attempts to do just that . . .

A LITTLE LOVING

Gael Morrison

Jenny Holden fell in love with Matt Chambers, the local high school football star. When she fell pregnant, he didn't believe the baby was his. Now a pro player, he is back in town to attend the wedding of his best friend, who is also Jenny's boss. And when he sees Jenny's son Sam, the boy's parentage is unquestionable. Jenny, now a widow, knows all Sam wants is a father — his real father. But can she trust the man who once turned his back on them?